THE DRAGON PRINCE'S MAGIC

THE ROYAL DRAGONS OF ALASKA
BOOK FIVE

ELVA BIRCH

Copyright © 2022 by Elva Birch

All rights reserved.

ROYAL DRAGONS OF ALASKA

This book is part of the Royal Dragons of Alaska series. All of my work stands alone (always a satisfying happy ever after and no cliffhangers!) but there is a story arc across books. This is the order the series may be most enjoyed:

>The Dragon Prince of Alaska (Book 1)
>The Dragon Prince's Librarian (Book 2)
>The Dragon Prince's Bride (Book 3)
>The Dragon Prince's Secret (Book 4)
>The Dragon Prince's Magic (Book 5)
>The Dragon Prince's Betrayal (Book 6)

Subscribe to Elva Birch's mailing list and join her in her Reader's Retreat at Facebook for sneak previews and news!

To everyone who marches to their own beat.

Different isn't less.

CHAPTER 1

Katy didn't notice that anything was wrong until the barista pushed her coffee across the counter and backed away cautiously instead of joking and flirting like she usually did. She turned to find two royal guards flanking her, a tall burly blond guy and a petite black-haired woman who was actually much more intimidating than her big male counterpart.

"Oh," Katy said with an automatic flare of alarm. She didn't often see royal guards, and their crisp blue uniforms with gold and fur trim came with a certain amount of ingrained respect and intimidation.

She wracked her mind. Had she forgotten to pay for her latte? Parked wrong? Run a red light on her way here? Stolen a car?

The last ridiculous thought calmed her nerves with its absurdity. "Can I help you guys?" Maybe there was royalty in town and they were just clearing the riff-raff out of the cafe before the paparazzi got there. She craned her neck to see to the door, but none of the other customers were being hassled, and there was no sign of the crowd that would undoubtedly precipitate the entrance of one of the popular Alaskan princes. Especially in these tense times, with kidnappings, weddings, assassination attempts, and protests.

"The captain wants to speak with you, Miss Davis," the woman said briskly. "We're here to escort you to the guard station."

Katy stared at her, trying to figure out what the captain of the royal guard would want with her. "Oh my gosh, did I witness a crime? Is this about Mr. Angrew? He has really poor personal boundaries, but he's harmless, really."

"I don't know anything about Mr. Angrew," the guard said. "The captain wants to see you right away."

Katy was impressed by how carefully the guards inserted themselves into her personal space, not exactly touching her, but obviously trying to guide her towards the door.

Katy perversely turned back to tuck a dollar into the tip jar. "Thanks, Betsy! See you tomorrow!" Maybe if she suspiciously disappeared, Betsy would think to follow up on it the next day.

Betsy gave her a wan smile that suggested she would do nothing of the sort. Betsy seemed like the type that would nod and smile and not rock boats, and if people started quietly vanishing, she would probably convince herself that she'd never even known them. Katy sighed and told herself that only happened in movies anyway.

She pulled up the hood of her parka and let the guards herd her outside, but although she had expected to walk the block to the guard station, there was a big black sedan waiting at the curb; it would have been blocking traffic if there had *been* any traffic. The burly guy opened the door for her and Katy cast one last, desperate look around before she obediently got in. "Do I scoot over for you?" she asked Mr.

Burly-and-Quiet as he held the door for her. "I've never been kidnapped before."

"We're not kidnapping you, ma'am!" The woman had come around to the far door and took a seat on the bench across the car from Katy as Mr. Burly shut the door and got in the front. They had a driver who took them through one intersection to the guard station.

Katy was pretty sure they spent as much time getting in and out of the car as they did driving. Downtown Kenai was not really that impressive or overly large.

She'd been inside the guard station twice before, once as a kid in high school doing a job learning day, and once to pick up a truant student. But she had never before been whisked through security (which seemed much tighter than she remembered either time) to a back room with a mirror that was absolutely a one-way window.

She really was going to be interrogated, Katy realized with a thrill of excitement. She couldn't imagine what she would know that would be of importance to the royal guard. She was a private teacher, specializing in special needs and one-on-one tutoring, mostly paid by charity grants. She didn't have a lot of money or prestige, and no connections to speak of. Her family was made up of long-time Kenai residents who had never been arrested, though her twin sister, Emaline, had gotten a citation once for jaywalking and several warnings for speeding.

"Do I get a phone call?" she asked Miss All-Business. Miss All-Business ignored her and left the room, looking cross.

Mr. Burly offered her a gruff cup of coffee. Katy raised her latte cup and wiggled it at him. "I'm good, thanks."

He followed Miss Business out.

She was nursing the last drops of her latte by the time the captain came in, and Katy stood up at attention without thinking twice about it.

She'd seen the captain in the news, of course, and she was pretty sure that the woman had never smiled in her life. Captain Luke didn't look young, but there wasn't a single crease on her smooth, golden-skinned face. The only lines on her face were the ones tattooed there, three vertical marks on her chin that were a callout to her Native culture.

"You may sit," the captain said, settling into a chair opposite from her. "You're probably wondering why I've called you here."

Katy dropped back down into her chair, far less gracefully. "You could say that, yes! I'll admit I'm rather wild with curiosity." She wished that she'd saved some of her latte, because it would have been comforting to have some to drink, and also because she needed to use the facilities now.

Captain Luke had been carrying a briefcase that she could probably take down a moose with and she opened it to take out a little packet of papers. "I cannot tell you more until you sign this non-disclosure form."

Katy took the stack of papers that Captain Luke passed across the desk. It was six pages, stapled, full of dense legal language. "Are you sure this is a non-disclosure contract?" she said skeptically. "It's not a confession to something I didn't do?"

If she hadn't been watching Captain Luke's face, Katy would never have caught the tiny flicker of a smile that twitched one corner of her mouth. Maybe there was a sense of humor under there!

"I assure you, it is a very standard non-disclosure form. It is only to protect both parties if you choose not to accept our offer."

Katy took the pen that the guard offered and hesitated over the pages only a moment before she flipped to the last page and signed her name with a flourish. To her astonishment, her signature burned on the page for a moment and then turned a glossy green.

Magic.

She guessed that she wouldn't be capable of violating the terms of the contract now if she tried.

She'd always known about magic. Her grandmother told her quiet stories about the secret casters who lived among them, and a little girl two houses over had sworn Katy to secrecy and then shyly showed her that she could shift into a domestic cat. Katy had immediately used her abilities to orchestrate the theft of treats from her mother's kitchen, and it was probably just as well that the girl had moved away shortly after that, before Katy could set more ambitious plots into action.

Until recently, magic and shifting had all been very hush-hush, swept under the rug and kept close to the chest. Almost everyone knew someone who knew someone who could write a laborious spell for removing an unsightly wart or shift into an animal. But it was easier by far to get a wart removed at the clinic, and people were generally too polite to go spying into backyards to bother about their neighbor's uncommon grazing method of lawn care.

It didn't really play a role in the day-to-day Internet and pay-the-bills life of the modern kingdom of Alaska. No one spoke out loud about it, or really acknowledged it. It was kept comfortably fiction, fantasized in popular media, with just enough truth to ring as an inside joke to those who knew.

Lately, however, it had started making the news, and not in a good way.

While some of the articles were dispassionate accounts of improbable things, the catchier headlines were spinning the events as *evil* and *orchestrated by demons*. There was talk of toppling the corrupted governments of the Small Kingdoms, and some of the capital cities had even had riots. Several of Katy's quietly magical neighbors had gotten jumpy and afraid, and everyone was suspicious of everyone else, eyeing each other and watching for unexplainable acts.

Mainstream newspapers glossed over this news, gentling it considerably, but the Internet was sizzling with the drama. Every day seemed like a new revelation, complete with cellphone footage.

Katy didn't know much about how media corporations and government worked, but she knew unrest when she saw it, and she could tell that they were scrambling to cover it up—and rapidly losing ground.

She still wasn't sure what any of that had to do with her. *She* was about as magical as a moose nugget.

"Do you follow the news much, Miss Davis?"

Was it a trick question? "A little? I mean, I don't read the newspaper cover to cover or anything, but I'm on Facebook and catch the important headlines, probably?" Katy had a feeling that her answer had not covered her with glory.

"You are aware that Prince Kenth has a daughter?"

That had *definitely* made the rounds of her Facebook feed. "Yes." The daughter had apparently even been *kidnapped* briefly, and Katy marveled that she now had that in common with a princess.

"Based on your unique qualifications and exemplary record, you have been chosen to come to the palace in Fairbanks and tutor her, along with a selection of other students at the castle who have a range of special needs. There will be other duties as assigned."

Katy blinked across the table. "I have some students here..." she started. The idea was a little thrilling, and she could not help but think of hot romance novels featuring princes and nannies.

"Yes," Captain Luke cut her off. "You have six part-time

tutoring students through the school district, ranging from first through eighth grade, two of them diagnosed with ADHD, one with impulse issues. Your contract is month-to-month and has not yet been renewed for February. We have a qualified candidate ready to step into this position if you are vetted through our process."

Katy wondered if she should feel bad about having her current career simplified in such an unflattering way. "If you have a qualified candidate, what do you need me for?" she asked, before she could remind herself that she'd probably make it further in the hiring process if she was more diplomatic.

"We have examined your background quite thoroughly, and decided that your range of special skills is exactly what we need. Your references have already been contacted. Room and board will be included in your salary, as well as a generous stipend. We'd require your immediate employment."

"This feels a bit like a mafia offer," Katy said frankly. "Too good to refuse." Her Chicago mobster accent was terrible.

Katy was watching the corner of her mouth, but either Captain Luke had suppressed her tell, or she wasn't amused.

The idea was honestly thrilling. To live in the palace and teach a *princess*. To rub elbows with royalty and stop wondering if she was dead weight to her sister because she couldn't really cover a valid share of her rent or groceries. She wouldn't have to worry about the expense of copies or supplies, or beg parents for field trip transport.

And Katy couldn't discount her wistful desire to step into a fairy tale and fall in love with a handsome prince.

There was something else, too. It was something deeper, like a compass pull that was urging her to say yes, to go *there*, to do *that*. Her grandmother had always encouraged her to listen to those whispers of instinct, and this was more like a dull roar or the tug of a strong river current.

"I'm in," she said.

A little shiver of anticipation sizzled through her. Whatever else happened, it probably wouldn't be *boring*.

CHAPTER 2

Raval made himself stop drumming his fingers, bored and restless.

The semi-regular formal family meetings had swelled with the distracting influx of extra people. What had been short, to-the-point meetings with five of the six brothers and Captain Luke now included a handful of his brothers' mates, and sometimes Drayger, the bastard prince of Majorca, if the topic required his expertise. (Raval personally thought he often overestimated his own necessity, but it didn't bother him *nearly* as much as it bothered Captain Luke.)

Toren, now crown prince despite being the youngest, had been firm about Carina joining them, to Fask's annoyance. Carina had then insisted that the other mates be included, since they still weren't certain which of them was actually going to be queen when the dust settled. With Kenth back now, apparently to stay, and *his* mate added to the mix, the informal dining room was full. Add in the restless state of Small Kingdoms these days, and the meetings were agonizingly long on top of that.

Raval forced himself to focus on Captain Luke's words,

and not just on the uncomfortable closeness of people around him and the stuffiness of the air in the room.

"I have it on very good authority that the traitor we are looking for is not a dragon," she said shortly. "Which basically eliminates only the people in this room."

Carina and Tania, the only occupants of the room other than Captain Luke who *weren't* dragon shifters, exchanged wry looks. Raval assumed that they got a free pass because, besides being respectively the mates of Toren and Rian, they didn't seem dangerous. Carina was slight, if scrappy, but Tania, battling chronic illness, usually walked with a cane and didn't look capable of the betrayal in question.

It also explained why Drayger had been included in today's meeting; he was the bastard son of the previous king of Majorca and a dragon shifter himself. Raval was inclined to take Captain Luke's statement at face value and accept that it meant he wasn't the traitor in question.

There was general political unrest and coordinated chipping away at the reputation of the various Small Kingdoms that was likely incited by magical means by a madwoman, Amara, who seemed determined to break the Compact that defined their authority and applied logical restrictions to magic itself. She was power-hungry and ruthless, and she controlled a widespread cult that was desperate to follow her cause.

And one of those followers was now somehow in the castle itself, and had attempted to kidnap Kenth's daughter.

"What manner of good authority?" Fask suspiciously wanted to know.

"The Compact herself," Luke said. "As unexpected as that is to consider." This caused a murmur of speculation.

Raval still wasn't sure what he thought about the recent revelation that the Compact was more than an elaborate spell. It had transcended to a sentient being at some point in

THE DRAGON PRINCE'S MAGIC

history, specifically a white-haired woman that they had all considered a spirit of the Alaskan royal castle. It unsettled him, the idea of magic manifesting itself, claiming self-awareness and individuality.

It made him question all the possibilities of his own magic, particularly of his longest-running project. Would it ever have the capacity to divest itself of *his* intentions?

He comforted himself with the reminder that his work was an order of magnitude less complicated than the Compact, which was a seven-hundred-page epic in very tiny print, written by casters that made his humble skills pale in comparison. His hobby car was not going to be demanding *citizenship* anytime soon.

"Can we trust her?" Fask wanted to know.

"How can we not?" Kenth countered. "The Compact is the structure of our entire civilization. It is the backbone of our authority."

Raval was fond of Kenth, but he wasn't fond of the conflict that had followed him home. Fask and Kenth had not outgrown their childhood habit of constantly butting heads. If Raval thought that Kenth had mellowed considerably since meeting his mate Mackenzie, it didn't keep the two oldest brothers from continuing their tiresome long-standing rivalry and antagonism.

Captain Luke neatly diffused the challenge. "I have been consulting with the Compact for many years when we considered her a fae spirit of the castle. I do not doubt her sincerity and I trust her completely. I'm confident that she would tell us more, if she could, but there are…constraints."

There were always constraints.

Magic was a tricky game of intention, and the Compact was the trickiest of all, a tangled legal document like a computer program of if and then statements. On the surface, it was a convoluted treaty between eleven nations. But underneath that facade was a maze of logic and rules, each one specific and ironclad. Mates were part of the Compact, casting a spell on two people to be the next monarchs of each of the Small Kingdoms.

Well, it was *supposed* to be only two. Raval cast a look down the table at Tray and Leinani. They were holding hands like they never wanted to let go of each other, like they were afraid they would lose each other if that contact ended. Tray had been the third brother tapped with a mate, and Kenth had followed closely.

For centuries, the Compact had chosen an oldest son or daughter, and paired them with mates that would continue the lines without question. It had been easy to spin the pairings for the public as unexpected love matches, because the Compact itself made it so easy for them to actually fall in love. Not only did it set them up to meet, it also exposed them to all of each other's feelings and the glorious potential of their match.

It sounded absolutely hideous to Raval. His own feelings were quite enough, thank you.

And now, not only were the mates—in Raval's opinion—a little unusual, there were *four* of them in one royal family. Two of them, Carina and Tania, were common-born Americans, and Tania was medically frail. Mackenzie was an escapee from Amara's cult, and a magical anomaly. As royalty herself, only Leinani was the slightest bit queenly—and the Compact had chosen the brother least likely to rule well for her mate, the troublemaker Tray.

Kenth and Fask were still arguing about whether or not the Compact was a reliable source of information, and Raval was pretty sure that at this point it was just because Fask didn't want to concede anything to Kenth.

Raval wondered if he could get away with just leaving the meeting.

THE DRAGON PRINCE'S MAGIC

Toren cleared his throat. "So, ah, Captain Luke, if you could let us know if you find anything else, that would be great. Is there any other business?"

Fask and Kenth stopped glaring at each other and settled back in their seats.

Captain Luke's face always looked serene, but Raval guessed that she was irritated. "I'll continue my investigation. We have selected a candidate for teaching the children. She's an Alaskan citizen, specializing in primary school education with certification in special needs. Her background check was clear and her references glowing; she's practically perfect. She has accepted the position and will be arriving today." She glanced at Kenth. "Kenth has conditionally approved her to teach Dalaya as well."

"All of Kenth's approval is conditional," Fask muttered, but he waved her on.

"The royal caster will be resetting the perimeter privacy spell today, so please avoid the inner courtyard until late afternoon."

All spells fade, Raval thought. And all meetings eventually ended.

Raval wasn't particularly fond of the business portion of these assemblies, but he liked the mingling before and after even less, and he dodged out of the room as quickly as he could when Fask formally released them. He breathed a sigh of relief when he made it out to the hallway, and then an even deeper one when he got to the outer door of the castle.

He didn't bother with a coat—as a dragon shifter, the cold didn't really bother him, and it was a short, brisk walk to his sanctuary, the detached garage with his workshop.

He was greeted at the door by a puppy.

"You are not supposed to be here," he told it.

It was one of Tray's latest dogsled puppies, a squishy-looking, big-pawed husky with ears that were far too large for its face and black masking around its eyes that made it look like it was wearing eyeliner. Its tail hadn't fluffed out yet, it was just a white-tipped whip that was thumping against the garage door.

"Go away," Raval tried, but apparently that sounded like *let's play*. It fell to its elbows and growled happily, pouncing forward for a loose shoelace on Raval's boot.

"You should be in the kennel. Go get Tray! Or Nathaniel!"

The puppy cocked his head up at him like it was trying desperately to understand, and for a moment, Raval had some hope.

That hope was swiftly dashed when the puppy charged forward again, falling on Raval's feet to wrestle with the offending boot.

Raval sighed and looked longingly at the door to his refuge. He couldn't just let the dog run wild, and he certainly wasn't going to let it inside with him, so he'd have to figure out how to get it back to where he belonged by brute force.

It wasn't very big, but it was apparently not used to being carried, and when Raval swept it up into his arms, it struggled and started vocalizing with the talking-howling sounds that were common to its breed.

When it realized that Raval wasn't going to let it go, it didn't stop struggling, but it did change its tactic to *licking* him.

It was *still* licking him when he met Nathaniel, the dog handler, halfway to the dog runs and close enough that the dogs were barking in greeting.

"Ah," Nathaniel said, reaching to take the wriggling canine. "You'd think that Lancelot was Trixie's whelp, not Phoebe's! He's managed to escape from every collar and crate we've put him in."

Raval grunted conversationally and was happy to pass off the drooly puppy and flee back to his garage hideout.

CHAPTER 3

The Royal Alaskan Castle was everything that Katy had imagined it would be from her studies of the photographs on the Internet...and a lot of things that she hadn't.

"That tickles," she giggled, her arms wide as the brisk, scowling captain of the Royal Guard frisked her.

Once again, Captain Luke didn't look amused, and she was very efficient in her search, squeezing every pocket and fold of cloth as she inspected Katy from her chin to her bare feet—her shoes had already been confiscated. Even Katy's thick, curly hair had been checked, like she might be hiding contraband or explosives there.

Katy's luggage and her large purse were being completely dismantled on a table just inside the palace entrance, zippers wanded, and there were no fewer than six giant burly uniformed men holding a weird array of weapons ranged around the room in tactical spots. Most of them had rather alarming-looking guns, but a few had...carved spears?

Were they formal trappings, or were they magic? It was weird to see it so out in the open.

"Just books," she called to one of the luggage inspectors, who was apparently invested in opening and flipping through each page individually. A bookmark fell out of one of them and the man fumbled the book and lost the place. "That's okay," she said kindly, pitching her voice to carry. "I've read it before."

If they were amused when they found her sister's Princes of Alaska Autograph Book, they gave no sign of it.

The captain of the guard had apparently finished her investigation of Katy herself, and her shoes, which had been carefully inspected and checked with what looked like a blacklight, were returned. "I apologize for the invasion of your privacy," the captain said, and Katy was inclined to believe that it was genuine.

"It seems like a lot of fuss for a nanny," Katy said with a sunny smile as she slipped her shoes back on. "Do I get to meet my students now?"

The captain did not smile in return. "There's more. This way, please."

Katy attempted to make conversation as she hopped a few steps to settle a stubborn shoe onto her foot. "I'm really looking forward to this. It's always exciting starting something new."

The captain didn't answer and Katy wryly thought that her sister Emaline would love to take lessons in subtle exasperation from her.

Down a long hall, they were met by a woman with strawberry-blonde hair pulled back from her face. She had a little halo of disobedient hairs around her features, which Katy intimately understood.

"I'm Teacher Katy," Katy said. She was vaguely aware of the guards pulling back to the end of the hall, and the captain disappearing altogether.

"I'm Mackenzie," the woman replied, not offering a title.

THE DRAGON PRINCE'S MAGIC

Katy guessed that she was the assistant she'd been promised. There was just a moment of hesitation before her name and the hand that she extended for a handshake, like she wasn't really sure of her own authority.

That was something else that Katy completely understood, and she shook Mackenzie's hand with all the warmth and friendliness that she could muster. There was a hulking man behind her, and Katy assumed by his uniform and short hair that it was yet another guard, until he stepped forward with a very wary handshake and introduced himself. "I am Kenth. Dalaya is my daughter."

His voice was all threat and warning. This was the most mysterious of the royal Alaskan brothers, recently returned to the palace with an unexpected daughter that the tabloids speculated about wildly. No one knew who her mother was.

Katy was pretty good at reading people, especially the way that they interacted with each other. It was a useful skill with non-verbal children, but she thought she didn't need any particular skill to recognize that these two were keenly *aware* of each other and deeply attached. If Mackenzie wasn't actually Dalaya's mother, she might as well be.

So much for her wild fantasies about coming to the Alaska palace and living out a melodramatic novella about a prince and his nanny! She found Kenth a little too intimidating, anyway; she liked a guy she could cuddle with, and he looked way too prickly for that.

Katy kept herself from curtseying, and instead shook his hand firmly and gave him a bold grin. "I'm looking forward to meeting Dalaya."

"These are your rooms," Mackenzie said, and one of the guards opened double doors onto a suite straight out of a movie and carried in her luggage.

There was a sitting room, with plush furniture and thick rugs. Katy was tempted to take off her shoes and wriggle her toes in it. The ceilings were ridiculously high, and the windows overlooking a snowy garden were enormous and framed in heavy, velvet curtains. She couldn't help but wonder how much it must cost to keep it all heated. There was a fireplace with a small, crackling fire behind glass, but it seemed more for atmosphere than warmth.

There was a private bathroom with gleaming fixtures, and a bedroom big enough to waltz in. Her luggage was placed next to a towering wardrobe, looking very small and shabby indeed.

Mackenzie, Kenth, and Captain Luke all followed Katy in and patiently waited while she exclaimed over how nice everything looked and petted the soft throw over the back of the couch.

There was a tension to them that didn't really seem appropriate to showing a new live-in teacher around and Katy turned to face them after a very brief tour. "Will I meet Dalaya now?"

"There are some things you need to know first," Kenth said gravely. "Your agreement mentioned extra children."

"Yes," Katy said, looking between them and then glancing back at the carefully blank expression of the Captain of the Guard. "The contract was for all the children of the castle. I presume that the staff has some children that you would like to have educated along with your daughter? I wholeheartedly agree with that plan and understood that was a part of my employment. A classroom of variable ages is always challenging, but I'm quite prepared for the range of educational needs."

She laughed, rather nervously, because no one was offering any more information or answers and she was probably rambling. "I wouldn't want to do more than a dozen, I should say, and that is probably testing the limits of how interested and involved you can keep them, but there's an assistant, I believe?" She glanced at Mackenzie with questions in her eyebrows. "It kind of depends on the individual children. I've had successful groups of twenty, spread out over six grades, and a half dozen that were too much of a handful to manage myself. I really won't know until I meet them and get started and run my assessment."

Yes, she was definitely rambling. Katy made herself shut her mouth before she could apologize for a failure she hadn't even realized yet.

"There are eleven children, they are probably nine or ten, except for Randal, who is thirteen or fourteen, and Dalaya, who is five. They are...all very *unique*," Mackenzie said softly. She exchanged a look with Kenth that sizzled with unspoken communication.

"Special needs were mentioned," Katy said, starting to wonder what she was getting into. Why wasn't Mackenzie sure of most of their ages? She hadn't gotten an individual workup of the students, and everything was so shrouded in secrecy. Were they royal diplomatic refugees? Were they *mutants* or *aliens*? At this point, nothing was too bizarre to consider.

"They're magic," Kenth said flatly.

"Oh, is that all?" Katy was almost disappointed. *Aliens* would have been particularly exciting. "Casters or shifters?"

If they were surprised that she knew that much about magic, they didn't show it. Probably, that had been part of her background check.

"They are all casters," Mackenzie said. "We don't actually know how much they can do on their own because they were always used with a magical focusing stone."

"Used?" Katy didn't mean to pounce, but the way Mackenzie said the word was so layered with meaning and distaste that her imagination leapt to the worst.

"They were kidnapped by a woman named Amara, the

leader of a cult called the Cause, and they were forced to write magical spells." Kenth's hands were on Mackenzie's shoulders, and she was even more pale than she'd started.

That was even more dire than Katy had conjectured. "Kidnapped? Forced to write spells? Were they *hurt?*"

"They weren't hurt," Mackenzie said with an undertone of steel. "But they were denied their childhood."

"Where are their parents?" Katy demanded, completely forgetting that she was dealing with royalty and it was her first day of work and she should maybe be a *little* reserved. "Shouldn't that be the priority here? To return them to their families?"

"The spell stone muddled their memories," Mackenzie said, and Kenth growled, "Don't think we haven't tried."

"We don't know where they came from," Mackenzie explained. "I was never told where Amara got them and none of them remember any details that are helpful. She wouldn't have taken them from places they would be missed and draw attention to her."

Katy filed that information without judgment; clearly Mackenzie had been a part of the organization, and she just as clearly had repudiated it. If the royal family could trust her now, probably Katy could, too.

Mackenzie went on. "They're very attached to each other now. I think we'd have trouble separating them even if we somehow found their families."

Katy gave a humorless chuckle. "Okay, well, this probably falls under the part in the job description with *other duties as needed*. You know from my resume that I've dealt with children who came from tough situations, so I'm not going in completely blind. Other than being kidnapped, traumatized, and having their memories wiped, is there anything else I should know about them before we get started?"

Mackenzie exchanged a look with Kenth and when she

THE DRAGON PRINCE'S MAGIC

looked back at Katy, her eyes were full of hope. Katy thought that she might have just passed a test more intense than the security check at the palace entrance or the not-a-kidnapping that she'd endured in the Kenai royal outpost.

"Dalaya will not be joining the class yet," Kenth said. He still sounded quite cool, but he seemed marginally less prickly, at least. "She is much younger than the others, only five, but I will require that you spend time each week tutoring her separately."

Katy nodded sagely. "It would be challenging to incorporate her into a class of kids so much older than her. We'll have plenty of time for free play that she is welcome to join us for."

"She's not to draw," Kenth said flatly.

Katy might have wondered if it was a joke, at first, but she was beginning to suspect that there wasn't much to laugh about here. Mackenzie and Kenth both looked utterly grim again.

"No...drawing?"

"Dalaya can do chaos magic. She doesn't need the structure of a written spell, but it does seem to be funneled through her art, and it can...be very unpredictable and dangerous." Mackenzie looked down at her own hands. There was definitely a story there, and Katy was wild to ferret it out, but she reminded herself to be patient.

"No drawing," Kenth growled.

Katy blinked at them. "Five is very young to work magic at all." She didn't know much about magic, but she thought it took more maturity than that, and an ability to write well, which was a stretch for most five-year-olds.

"She was...tinkered with," Mackenzie said, and there were even more hints to her own story in her voice.

"I will be sure to keep her under careful observation," Katy said warmly, deciding not to pry. "We should discuss exactly what we can do with her education. It's unconventional to use methods of teaching that don't rely on writing and drawing, but there are other ways to build fine motor skills and learn letters. Is there anything else I should know about Dalaya?" She didn't want to appear impatient, but the check-in process at the castle had already taken much longer than she expected, and she was honestly dying to meet her new students. Even if they *weren't* aliens.

Mackenzie and Kenth shared another of those long looks full of meaning and it was Kenth who offered, "She's a dragon shifter."

There was a hint of a smile at the corner of his mouth, but Katy didn't think that he was the type to tease her. She smiled back anyway and nodded slowly. *Why not,* she figured.

Mackenzie was nodding as well, and she finally said, "We should go meet the kids and get you settled."

"Yes, please!" Katy said. She paused to get the introductory workbooks from her luggage, glad that she'd decided to bring extra copies after all.

She would ask Kenth for an autograph for her sister's book at a better time.

* * *

THE SCHOOLROOM WAS JUST down the hall from Katy's suite, past another guest room that they briefly stopped at that had been converted for the children as a dormitory. The two bedrooms off the sitting room were for the boys and girls, with bunkbeds and dressers for each of them. It looked like it had all been hastily decorated with a mis-match of popular children's themes, with posters up between framed classical paintings that Katy suspected were originals. All of the toys looked crisply new, like they were straight out of packaging.

"You won't be responsible for their nighttime care or

required to give them constant supervision," Mackenzie clarified. "Their education will be in your hands, but Mrs. James will attend to their meals and non-classroom duty."

Not really a *nanny*, then. Katy was a little relieved. A dozen children with such traumatic pasts to catch up on curriculum was already a lot, and it sounded like a full-time job without adding the rest of their care.

They went down the hall again, to another set of rooms that had obviously been guest suites. This room had been set up with desks and whiteboards. There were computers and scientific equipment and games, easels and art supplies. Untouched reams of paper were stacked at work tables, with cups of sharpened pencils and shelves of books. Katy would have put money on the fact that not one of the whiteboard markers would be dry. The boards themselves had a virgin whiteness to them that never lasted past a first use.

At any other point in her life, Katy would have been in raptures over how well supplied they were, at the thrill of having so much new, top-of-the-line equipment to work with.

But she had eyes only for the children waiting for her.

They were all sitting quietly, not fidgeting at all or playing with the supplies at their desks. It was eerie and more than a little sad. Katy felt her heart melt.

She started with her usual introduction to a new classroom, telling them a bullet-points version of her life first. "I'm from Kenai," she said. "It's a little town down on the coast with a lot of trees and salmon. Have you eaten salmon?"

It was Alaska, so she usually had a hand or two up, but she was surprised to find that none of them actually had…and she was further intrigued by the variety of races among the kids as they went around the class introducing themselves. Paige appeared to be a Pacific Islander, and Taxina looked very

Slavic. Lon was clearly Latin. Cindy was so sepia skinned that she made Katy's interracial brown skin look pale, with deep brown eyes and springy curls like Katy's. Jamie was a redhead who looked a great deal like a miniature Mackenzie, and Prit was probably middle-eastern, maybe Mediterranean. Jessica and Danny were probably of white European decent, and Jin was Asian—Korean, by Katy's guess.

They all spoke English, but some of them had thick accents and it might be their second language. Katy made a mental note about which ones might need some extra help with reading.

Cindy seemed to be the unspoken ringleader of the group, always speaking first and checking in with the others.

"I brought a fun workbook for each of you," Katy said once introductions were done. "I want you to answer each of the questions as best you can, and if you don't know an answer, you can just skip right over it. There's no grading, don't worry!" Did they even know what grading *was?* "This will help me know what to teach you and what you most want to learn. On the back page, I want you to draw me a picture of your favorite thing in the whole world." She dropped her voice to conspiratorial tones. "My favorite thing is ice cream."

Several of the children smiled, and Cindy giggled, but they remained very still and contained at their desks. No one swung their legs or rocked back in their chairs or whispered with their neighbors. Katy passed out a workbook and repeated their names back to them in turn, memorizing each one as she let them choose a pen color from her hand.

Don't let Dalaya draw, she reminded herself. It all felt very surreal, and she almost felt like she had an echo of her own feelings in her head, distant and separate.

It was only after they were bending their heads over the

task, unexpectedly focused and obedient, that it occurred to Katy that this might be too similar an exercise to the description Mackenzie had given her of their labor for Amara—writing on command. She would definitely have to re-examine her lesson plan and put more of an emphasis on playing and cooperative learning exercises. Not that her lesson plan so far was much more than *roll with the punches* and *play it by ear*.

She pulled Mackenzie out of earshot and sat with her on a little couch to the side. "Is this all of them, except for Dalaya?" Ten seemed like a number that Katy could handle. Had Mackenzie counted Dalaya in her count of eleven? They were all very well-behaved. Maybe a little *too* well-behaved. It hurt her heart to think that they'd been kidnapped and used.

"Randal isn't here," Mackenzie said. "He's the oldest, about fourteen, and we suspect he's on the spectrum. He reads very well and loves history, but he finds it hard to deal with people."

Katy knew the kind of hesitation that came with trying to navigate talking about neurodivergent children. Terms came in and out of favor, and different people faced different challenges with different descriptors. All that Katy herself really cared about was that it clearly came from a place of loving and trying to understand.

"Does he have a formal diagnosis?" Katy asked.

Mackenzie shook her head. "No. They haven't been free from Amara for very long, and I didn't want to stress him out if we didn't have to. Are you, ah, licensed for that?"

"I'm not a doctor," Katy said, shaking her head. "Nor a behaviorist. I'm not qualified to make any official calls."

"Do we need to?" Mackenzie asked. "Is it beneficial to have a name for it? I don't really know how this works."

"It can be comforting to know," Katy said candidly. "But it really depends on the person. Randy...it was Randy, right?"

"Randal."

"Randal." Katy committed the name to memory. "Even with a diagnosis, kids are so individual. I wouldn't be doing much more with it than using it as a place to start to figure out what he likes and how he learns. Usually a diagnosis opens important doors for financial assistance, but if he's living in a palace, probably he doesn't have that problem."

Mackenzie chuckled, as Katy had meant her to, and she could see that the woman was starting to thaw even more as they talked.

"Does he disrupt the other children?" Katy wanted to know.

"Oh, no," Mackenzie assured her. "They love him very much and understand that he needs different things than they do. They're terribly protective, and they know that sometimes he doesn't like loud things or lots of smells. They look out for him, distract him if there's yelling, hug him if he's shaking."

"They're very quiet," Katy observed. Each of the children was very dutifully working on their assessment. There was still no whispering or restlessness. They didn't even look up from their work.

"Noisy children weren't encouraged in the Cause," Mackenzie said grimly. "We've—they've—been loosening up, believe it or not, and the princes get them to play video games or out in the snow sometimes, but this is their usual response to authority. I think that..."

Katy caught her wary look and did her best to look both interested and trustworthy. There were huge secrets here, and she was dying to know them.

"Amara had a focus stone that she used on them, to make them write spells faster. I wonder if it didn't put them a little out of step with regular time, if they aren't *older* than they actually are."

"Time travel?" Katy might have known about magic, but time travel seemed a step too far.

"Not time *travel*, as such, but a certain amount of flexing of time as they experienced it." Mackenzie was looking thoughtfully at her hands.

"I didn't think that was possible," Katy said.

"A lot of things I didn't think were possible turned out to be," Mackenzie said. She looked up and must have seen the wild curiosity that Katy was doing a poor job of hiding.

"I'm a dragon, too," she said shyly. "I didn't know I was. My mother suppressed it when I was a child to protect me from Amara's meddling. And now I'm a dragon, and I have powers I never dreamed of. Wild magic, chaos magic, like Dalaya's, that doesn't follow the rules. It has a price, though. And these kids paid some of that."

Katy felt a pang of sympathy that included Mackenzie.

Katy caught herself looking at the door. "What about Ra-Randal?" she asked. The name didn't feel quite right in her mouth. There was something nagging at her, something absolutely undeniable, like there were bees in her shoes, trying to sting her into standing up. "Shouldn't we get him?" Katy wasn't sure why she would think she even knew where he *was*.

"He'll come out when he's ready," Mackenzie said reassuringly. "It takes him a little while to get used to new things, and I told him he didn't have to be here right at first. Give the other kids a chance to mob you first, and you two can meet on his terms."

Katy was happy to hear that. She knew a lot of people tried to force neurodivergent kids into the same molds as other kids, with very variable results, and she was glad to hear that she wouldn't have that kind of work to undo.

But it still felt like there were bees in her shoes.

She was pretty sure there wasn't actually anything in her shoes—they had been very thoroughly inspected—but Katy still knew that there was something she had to do, even if she wasn't exactly sure what it *was*. "I'm sorry," she said, standing. "I really feel like I have to go find him now. My grandmother always said that you should listen to these kinds of feelings. I'm sorry, it's a little hard to explain, if I could…just…" She flapped hands at the door desperately. "That way. I have to go that way."

Mackenzie stood, but didn't stop her, and Katy, bemused by herself, went to the classroom door. "I'll be back to answer any questions, sorry. I really, really have to go now."

Then she fell out into the hallway, waving in chagrin to the guards who fell into step. She couldn't even tell them where she was going.

CHAPTER 4

Raval came warily from the garage, glancing in both directions and pausing to listen for laughter. The castle was infested with children.

It wasn't just Kenth's little curly-haired demon daughter, with her shrill demands and enchanted pictures. There were about a dozen of the monsters living in the family halls while the search continued for their proper families or suitable foster care.

It wasn't that the children were particularly ill-behaved. In fact, Raval suspected that they were not nearly as wild and willful as children their age ought to be. They were generally quiet and out of the way, but Raval found them unsettling and had enough trouble understanding normal fully grown people. He didn't understand the social rules of children, and it didn't help that they didn't seem to know the rules, either.

Toren and Tray, in particular, seemed to think that the solution to that was to encourage them to mischief and activity, and had reverted to their own childhood. They led campaigns in the yard that made getting to the garage a hazard of shrieks and snowballs. If the weather was too terrible for human children, they slid around the halls in their socks, and rode down banisters without shame.

Raval didn't begrudge them their fun, but he didn't know what to do in the face of it, or how to speak to kids at all, so he preferred to avoid them altogether. He made it to the house unmolested and took the long way around to the front hall in order to skirt the halls they usually used.

He was unsuccessful in avoiding them altogether.

One of the young people was sitting on the stairs up to his rooms. It was the oldest one, Raval thought, a boy on the reluctant cusp of adulthood.

Raval might have made it safely past and up to his rooms, but the boy gave a noisy sigh of misery and Raval closed his eyes and dredged inside his chest for patience. This was a situation that called for empathy. These kids were refugees from a dangerous magic cult. They'd been forced to make spells—sloppy, dangerous spells—like they were in some kind of enchantment factory run on child labor and artifacts.

He just wished they were someone else's problem right now.

"Are you okay?" he asked gruffly.

The boy stared at him without response.

"I heard they were going to get you a teacher," Raval said, desperately grasping at conversational straws.

This, however, appeared to be the exact wrong thing to say.

"She won't like me," the boy said miserably. Randal was his name, Raval remembered suddenly. "And Mackenzie says I might have to go away, anyway."

"Why wouldn't the teacher like you?" Raval asked, trying to sound jovial. It took him a moment to recognize that the boy was still staring at him without looking away. That was the kind of thing that bothered most other people, and Raval had grudgingly learned not to do it himself in order to fit in, but he'd bet half his hoard that Randal wasn't entirely neurotypical.

Like Raval himself.

The sympathy he'd had to look for was all he felt now. It was a lot to face the world knowing that you were out of step with everyone else. But Raval was very sure about one thing. "They aren't going to hire a teacher that won't like you. Believe me, Fask will pick the very best of the best. She'll be a Mary Poppins, wait and see."

"What's a Mary Poppins?" Randal asked.

Raval thought he said it sullenly, but Raval rarely read emotion correctly into other people, so it probably wasn't. These kids hadn't been exposed to much modern media, so he assumed the question was genuine.

"Mary Poppins is practically perfect in every way," Raval quoted. "She's a magical nanny who comes to teach children to use their imagination. She was in a book before the movie."

"I'm magical," Randal said thoughtfully. "Is that Mary Poppins?"

A woman with bouncy black curls had just come around the corner at the bottom of the stairs and something inside of Raval seemed to snap into place.

Raval was used to being a few steps behind everyone else. He remembered people's names late in every conversation and laughed at jokes after they weren't funny anymore. He realized only now that his feeling of urgency when he left his garage sanctuary had not been to the purpose of evading children, but to being here, in this place, to meet this woman at this moment.

He examined her carefully, trying to decide what it was about her that appealed to him so completely. There was something about her mouth, about how red and full her lips were, something about her curly, dark hair. There was something about her figure—is that what books referred to as lush? There was something about her dancing brown eyes. There was something about all of her that was absolutely, undeniably…practically perfect.

"Well, hello," she said cheerfully. She looked a little confused, like she'd been expecting someone else and been pleasantly surprised. She *felt* a little confused, Raval realized. He could *feel* her reaction to him.

She was confused, and she was dazzled.

Raval actually had to look around, to make sure she wasn't looking at one of his brothers standing behind him.

"You're Raval, aren't you?" she said, sounding breathless. Feeling breathless. She bounded up the few steps separating them and extended her hand. "I'm Katy. I'm here…well, I thought I was here to act as a live-in nanny and teacher for a while, but I think I'm here to meet you. I'm sorry, that's the wildest thing, isn't it?"

"No," Raval said hesitantly. "It's not."

He realized belatedly that he was supposed to shake her hand, and he shyly slipped his hand into hers.

The touch of her skin on his was like electricity. But good electricity, warm and welcome. He could hold on to that hand for the rest of time. This was what he'd been put on this earth to do, to hold that hand and fall down into those eyes.

Fortunately, Katy actually knew how a handshake was supposed to go, and she gave his arm a cheerful couple of pumps and extracted herself before Raval could make it weird.

"I'm sorry," he said.

"For what?" Katy laughed. "Never apologize if you don't mean it."

She was so joyful, Raval thought. He'd never thought much about happiness, but this woman was his, he thought. His whole world was brighter and broader and safer. He was filled with relief and his dragon was whispering in his ear urgently.

He had to concentrate to make words out of the swirl of feelings inside him.

...our one! Our destiny! His dragon was always more certain of things that he was.

"Are you Katy Poppins?" Randal asked. Raval had nearly forgotten he was there.

Katy's laughter was like music, Raval thought. Really good music. "I can be," she said kindly. "You must be Randal. I'm looking forward to teaching you and I hope we'll get along well."

But she turned back to Raval even as she spoke, drawn like a magnet. The same magnet that was drawing Raval to her.

Raval didn't always trust his own conclusions. He knew that he saw the world a little differently than most people, and what seemed obvious to others was obtuse to him, just like things that he thought were completely undeniable seemed outside of the grasp of others' understanding.

This was not a conclusion he could deny.

"You're my mate," he blurted.

"Okay," Katy said cheerfully. "What's that?"

CHAPTER 5

In all of Katy's wild fantasies about meeting an Alaskan prince and becoming the nanny in a naughty book, she had never imagined it would be like this.

He was as beautiful as she'd thought he would be, but that wasn't much of a surprise; the Alaskan princes were plastered over the internet as sex symbols, and Raval lived up to every inch of that hype. Even his slightly cool, distant expression could not in any way make him look anything other than movie-star striking, and his body and his grace hit something primal in Katy. He was the only blond of the brothers, with soft, unruly hair and a scruff of a beard, like he couldn't be bothered to shave. It didn't do much to mask his magnificent jaw.

But more than that—much more!—Katy felt like she'd been dipped in sugar and set on fire. Even though his face was neutral, she somehow knew without a shadow of a doubt that he was absolutely alive for her, that her attraction to him was amplified back in spades, which was itself a heady and fabulous feeling.

And beyond that purely animal magnetism, Katy felt

overwhelmingly safe, like she'd known this guy for years, not just a few moments. Her whole chest felt full of affection for him, and unquestioning trust. And if she didn't know better, she'd say that she was feeling his emotions, too: interest, alarm, and bone-deep longing.

"You're my mate," Raval repeated unhelpfully.

"I know, you told me that," Katy said merrily, but there was an undercurrent of rising panic that she wasn't sure was hers or his. Was she enchanted? Was this some kind of mistake? "What does that *mean?*"

"I don't know," he said helplessly, and Katy was sure that the wave of frustration was his. No, maybe it was a little of hers, too.

He shook his head and backed away up a few steps so that Katy had to crane her neck to look up at him. "I don't know," he repeated. "But I have to go now. Right now. This isn't. I don't know."

And then he fled, leaving Katy alone with a confused Randal.

She wasn't much less confused herself. "That was very odd," she said out loud.

Whatever was going on in her head, with the swirling storm of emotions that weren't all hers, she was here for a job, and Randal was part of that. "Would you like to come back to the classroom with me?" she offered. Then, because it was an appealing idea, and because offering a concrete choice of two options was a very effective way of dealing with many children, whether they were neurotypical or not, she added: "Otherwise, we could just sit here on the stairs together for a little bit."

Randal looked hard at her and Katy wondered what she must look like from the outside, completely flustered and ridiculously keyed up after meeting Raval. She needed a cold shower and a stiff drink, and had to settle for pinching herself.

"I'd like to go back," he said after a moment.

"I hope you know the way," Katy said. "I got all sorts of turned around on my way here."

Randal proved to be the sort who enjoyed it when people put faith in him, and he happily led her back through her guards, who had been lingering at the far end of the hall to give an impression of privacy. Katy wondered how much they'd been able to hear.

Randal was greeted warmly by the other kids and willingly bent over the workbook she gave him. "I like history best," he told her shyly, when she gave her ice cream confession.

The children seemed to have thawed a little, and as they finished Katy's workbooks, she set them loose on the fun activities that were available to see how they would react to free play. They smiled and even laughed with her, and if their choices of entertainment were surprising—Cindy took a book on thermodynamics and Danny began sketching a fine technical rendering of the schoolroom with an impressive level of detail—they seemed sure-footed about what they liked to do, and considerably less afraid of her.

"Amara didn't let them read history," Mackenzie explained, when Katy retreated to the far side of the room with her again to avoid hovering too obviously while the last ones finished their assessments. "Not real history, anyway. Randal's been trying to make up for lost time since we got here." If she'd been shocked by Katy's abrupt departure and return, she didn't say as much.

Katy still wasn't entirely sure where Mackenzie fit in all of this, besides being clearly attached to Kenth and having *history* with an evil Cause, and being a dragon with wild magic, but she obviously felt responsible for the children, and her affection for them was unmistakable.

"The kids are great," Katy said sincerely. "They're remarkably well-adjusted considering everything that they've been through." Torture? Memory erasure? They might be older than they actually *were*? They didn't even have birthdays. It was mind-boggling. But more mind-boggling yet... "Mackenzie, what's a mate?"

Mackenzie's whole face softened, like she was suddenly remembering something so happy she couldn't help it. "It's a kind of magic," she said softly. "Part of the spell of the Compact."

"The Small Kingdoms treaty?" What did a bunch of dusty documents about preferred trade and mutual protection have to do with *feeling Raval's emotions*?

"The Compact is actually a spell." Mackenzie shook her head. "No, it's actually so complicated that it's more like a *person*, sort of like an artificial intelligence, with rational thoughts and purpose. It's—*she's*—part of the structure and limitations of all magic in our world." She gave Katy a very shrewd look, like she'd just figured out why Katy was asking the questions she was. "She selects a partner for the heir, or at least she's supposed to. Alaska has kind of an embarrassing number of them right now. Carina was called for Toren, Tania for Rian, Leinani for Tray, and..." she blushed rosy behind her freckles.

"You and Kenth," Katy guessed.

"You and Fask?" Mackenzie guessed in return.

Katy shook her head. "Raval," she said breathlessly.

Her cheeks heated, and they exchanged foolish smiles. "What does it mean, though?" she wanted to know. "Is it... like a love potion? Magic always fades, so are we going to wake up in a few days feeling like we over-indulged and got soul-hitched in Las Vegas? Can it be annulled?" Did she want it to be?

Mackenzie shook her head slowly as her smile faded to a thoughtful expression. "It's not like a love potion, precisely. It's more like it makes sure you meet, and gives you a glimpse of each other's feelings, as well as your possible *future* feelings."

"Yes, oh my gosh! I do have all these weird feelings that don't seem to be mine, and it's very unnerving." Katy felt a wave of relief...and abruptly wondered if Raval, somewhere else in the palace, felt it too. "It's a little wild to feel these things for someone I only barely met and it's very surreal. I worried that I was being, I don't know, controlled or something!"

"It doesn't replace free will," Mackenzie comforted her, as if she understood Katy's misgivings. Probably, if she'd gone through the same thing, she did. "It's just kind of...a dangling carrot. It's what could be, if you let yourself."

"Was it like that for you? What you thought you'd feel, you actually *did*, later? Er, do now?"

Mackenzie chewed on her lip. "I used to be immune to magic," she explained. "When it started out, only Kenth felt our bond and my feelings, I couldn't feel his at all. But later...something happened." Something major, Katy recognized, and she knew she was only getting part of the story. "By the time I could feel it, I was already crazy in love with the guy, and it wasn't a feeling of what could be, but what already was, like a weird echo. Everyone else says it was like that, that what they thought it could be, it actually became. Even when they didn't want it to."

"Why wouldn't someone want it to?" Katy asked incredulously. "This is the dream! The call of destiny! It's like a fairy tale happy ever after! Even if it's a little overwhelming at first!"

"Leinani came here to marry Fask," Mackenzie said. "She and Tray tried really hard not to fall in love. They were going to stay apart and try to outlast it, but Amara kidnapped them together and they did anyway."

"This Amara sounds like a real piece of work," Katy observed. "What with the kidnappings and controlling children to write magic spells." She was still itching to ask after Mackenzie's role in the whole thing. "I wasn't hired to be a princess. I'm a teacher. What exactly does this mean for me?"

Mackenzie's expression was grave. "It means you might be the next Queen of Alaska."

Katy knew this jolt of shock was entirely her own. Did that fall into the category of *other duties as assigned?*

CHAPTER 6

Raval stared out the window over the blue, snow-covered yard. It was marginally easier than staring in the other direction at the thrones clustered at one end of the hall.

He was concentrating so hard on the view, on how peaceful this visage was supposed to be, about what emotions he ought to be feeling, about which emotions were actually his, that he didn't notice Fask until his oldest brother tapped him on the shoulder.

"Earth to Raval," he said. "What's eating you?"

Eating him?

Was love supposed to *devour* him? Raval wondered. Was it supposed to consume him until there was nothing left? He abruptly thought that being eaten by Katy would not be unpleasant, and he was sure that there was a sex joke here that he should be chortling over. Tray would know that joke.

"The new teacher, Katy, is my mate," he said flatly. There was undoubtedly a conversational way to lead into something like that, but Raval didn't know what it was.

Fask stared at him.

"Are you...sure?"

"Yes." Whatever other doubts he had, like why on earth the Compact would choose a fifth brother and why that would be Raval, he could not deny the feeling of Katy under his skin, the pull that he felt towards her, or the tingle of magic that came with it. He could classify every one of his bizarre symptoms and stack them against the edicts of the Compact and his brothers' experiences with a perfect match. His dragon was completely convinced and had always been more sensitive to magic than Raval alone was.

The most *logical* solution was that Katy was his mate.

What that meant, of course, was quite a different question. "I don't believe this indicates that I'm intended to rule," Raval added. "Clearly, there's some...confusion in the code that has called five of us at all. It seems logical that you'll get a mate next, and perhaps there's some loophole that will make you king then. You're the only one who wants this."

Raval thought as he spoke that his statement wasn't quite accurate, because while he didn't want the *throne*, he couldn't imagine not wanting Katy.

As distasteful as he'd found the hypothetical idea of a mate, the reality of having her bound by magic in his heart was an amazing feeling of completion. She seemed to fill in all the weird little corners of his feelings where other people had personalities and he had to pretend to fit in.

But he'd long since learned that clarifying his point usually only caused more confusion, so he only held that realization close.

Fask clapped him on the shoulder, hard, and said, "Congratulations!" Was it a little brighter than it ought to be? Did he sound *angry*? Raval was a terrible judge of those kinds of things.

"What does this mean for the Renewal?" Raval wanted to know.

The Renewal was coming that summer, and it would refresh the Compact itself, part of a ceremony that reset the waning spell. Now, more than ever, they knew exactly how important that Renewal actually *was*. The Compact defined the structure of magic itself and kept it from running wild across the world in unbridled chaos.

"I have no idea," Fask said shortly.

"Who are we going to send?" Raval persisted, not sure if he'd asked the question correctly the first time.

"I don't know!" Fask snapped. "Toren is begging me to let him off, Rian is avoiding me, I wouldn't send Tray to represent us at any event more formal than a barroom brawl, and Kenth…" He didn't have to finish the sentence.

That left Raval. "I'm no diplomat," he protested.

"I wasn't *suggesting* you." Fask rubbed his face. "I'm sorry to sound short. It's just…"

Did he feel badly because he was the only brother who hadn't been chosen? It would match Raval's own observations about feeling left out.

"Maybe you just haven't been chosen *yet*," Raval offered. "It would certainly simplify things if you were. Rian and Toren both said that their dragons were sort of agitated a little while before they actually met. Maybe your dragon can tell if your mate is coming?"

Fask was quiet for long enough that Raval had time to cast back over what he'd said, analyzing whether it had been clear or not. It wasn't quite a direct question.

"Did your dragon tell you?" his brother finally asked.

Had his dragon been sort of nagging at him before he actually met Katy? Raval was used to ignoring things around him, and that sometimes included the dragon that shared his soul. Certainly, his dragon had *realized* what was happening well before Raval himself had. And dragons were considerably more sensitive to magic—both structured and natural—than humans were.

Fask was still looking at him and Raval thought that there was something sort of hungry or angry in Fask's face. But Raval wasn't sure which and didn't trust his own interpretation anyway, so he only shrugged. "Dragons aren't always very clear," he said.

"Except when they are," Fask said flatly.

Raval felt like maybe they were having two completely different conversations, which wasn't that uncommon for him.

"What do you want me to do?" Raval asked with a sigh.

"What can you do?" Fask scoffed. "You've been chosen, for better or for worse, and apparently, you're going to love her, whether you want to or not."

That should feel appalling, Raval thought, and it *didn't*. He didn't particularly like the implication that free will wasn't a factor, but he didn't mind the idea of loving Katy in the slightest. He wasn't sure how someone could be so full of life and joy without being overwhelming, but there was something about her gentleness that kept him from feeling crushed by her intensity.

Then it occurred to him that Katy might not feel the same way. She might not *want* to be attached to someone like him. He wasn't the easiest person to be around, and he could only imagine how uncomfortable the inside of his head might be to someone else. She didn't seem—or feel!—disappointed, but perhaps the mate bond was only sharing his emotions selectively. And when it was gone…

He was staring at his faint reflection in the glass and he could see Fask beside him, looking thin and wavery.

"I'm almost done with the car," he said abruptly. It was easier to think about that than let his mind wander down unpleasant paths.

Fask gave him a skeptical sideways look. "Seriously? After all this time? Are you ever going to tell us what it's supposed to do?"

"That's going to be difficult to do," Raval said wryly. "Because I'm not even sure myself."

CHAPTER 7

Mrs. James, a round gray-haired woman who looked like she'd stepped out of a novel as the sweet busy-body housekeeper—possibly one who solved flower-themed murder mysteries—was quick to assure Katy that she wasn't expected or required to go out with the kids and the princes to play in the snow later that afternoon.

"They're all dragons, so they can keep the poor things safe," she promised.

Katy remembered that Dalaya was supposedly a dragon shifter. Was the entire royal family? The indisposed king was sometimes called the Dragon King and his sons the Dragon Princes, but Katy had always supposed that they were fanciful titles, intended to inspire awe and respect. She had never guessed that they would be literal. There was magic, and then there was *fantasy*.

"In the meantime, your presence has been requested by the crown princess in the library before dinner."

"Oh, thank you, that sounds lovely." Katy wondered how much of a request it really was. After a day of travel and a new job, and a lot of surprises, and a whole lot of noise in her own head that wasn't her own, she didn't particularly want to sip wine with a bunch of snotty princesses in a room full of dusty books, but she also knew that she wasn't really in a position to deny a summons from a *crown princess.*

"I'll just tidy and freshen myself up first," she said.

Mrs. James took that as a perfectly acceptable answer and told her how to find the library when she was ready.

Then Katy was alone in the classroom for the first time.

She knew that there were guards just outside the door, of course, but the silence that followed Mrs. James' exit was blissful relief and Katy let herself sink down into one of the half-sized desk chairs and put her face in her hands.

Raval.

Mates.

Spells.

Raval.

Katy thought she'd probably have liked him without a spell to tell her his emotions and the affection she *might* have for him later, but she guessed that it would have been a lot harder to develop real feelings. He was absolutely *gorgeous*, but she probably would have crushed on him from a distance without even once considering that she had a snowball's chance in hell with him. She wouldn't have ever really committed her heart without some encouragement that she knew Raval would never have offered.

It was hard, now, to guess what she might have observed from him without the spell, but Katy thought that she would not have picked up on so much as a shred of attraction from him on his face or in his body language. Instead, she knew *exactly* how seductive he found her, how tender and warm he was inside, and it was absolutely *thrilling*.

And the future? She felt her own feelings from the *future*?

Could she trust this future that she was being shown and base her actions on the incredible feeling of familiarity and

THE DRAGON PRINCE'S MAGIC

affection and security that she felt when she thought of him? Common sense suggested that she was the architect of her own destiny, and if she repudiated the bond, she could orchestrate a whole new outcome.

But she didn't particularly want to reject Raval. Whether it was now-feelings or maybe-then-feelings, she was already fond of him and she knew without a single hesitation that it would wound him desperately if she did.

Besides, he was entirely *mancandy*, with a body like an athlete or a supermodel. Her own body's base reaction to him was probably absolutely nothing to do with the spell; he lit her on fire like no one she'd ever met had. He was all of her romantic fantasies and every daydream she'd ever had, in one handsome package.

And a prince of Alaska.

Remembering Mackenzie's pronouncement chilled her ardor.

It meant that she might be the next queen of Alaska.

Katy had a good imagination, but that was not a future she could picture for herself.

* * *

Mrs. James' directions to the library were straight-forward and Katy, leaving her guards at the door with a cluster of other bored men and women in uniform, went in without knocking. She had her chin high, ready to face down a room full of judgment and interrogation.

She was not expecting the library to have a full bar, or for the crown princess, Carina, to bounce up from her chair and throw her arms around Katy.

"She's had a really long day, Carina," Leinani chided her from an elegant wing-backed chair. "Let her get a drink and have a seat."

"I'm sorry," Carina said, letting Katy go to arm's length. "I am just so excited every time that there's another one of us, because that means I am *that* much less likely to have to be queen! Come have a drink and tell us all about you!"

Katy had to laugh, because Carina's casual manners were disarming, and because she was clearly having the same reservations about being royalty that Katy herself was.

"There's soda if you don't want alcohol," Tania said, gesturing to the bar. She was sitting in a fancy recliner that looked comfortable but didn't really match the rest of the décor. Her gorgeous ornate cane was hanging on the arm.

Mackenzie was already there, sitting in the middle of a leather loveseat, and she waved sheepishly. "Sorry," she said. "I told them before I thought that maybe you should do it yourself."

Katy brushed off her apology and went to the bar. "I'm sure it wouldn't have been secret for long," she said kindly.

The bar was well-stocked. "That's a good gin. Is there tonic?" There was actually a fancy *tap* for tonic, and Katy made herself a judiciously weak drink with a wedge of fresh lime. She didn't want to completely lose her head, what was left of it, but she could use a little bit of an unwind and she was pretty sure that she wasn't going to have a lot of opportunity for it once she started her teaching in earnest. Especially now that she was royalty. Or at least, royalty-in-waiting. Royalty-by-spell? Was she technically a *princess* now?

It was still all utterly unreal.

Mackenzie made room on the loveseat for her and Carina flopped into a wing-backed chair that matched Leinani's but managed to look completely inelegant by comparison. They each had fancy glasses, but Mackenzie's smelled like root beer.

Katy, recognizing this stage of a meet-and-greet, told

them the grown-up version of her backstory, growing up in the working-class fishing town of Kenai and working on boats in the summer when she wasn't teaching. It was ironic that she was the only one of them who was actually from the Kingdom of Alaska. "I originally thought I might go into social work," she said, "but teaching was my real calling, and...now I'm here."

"It's a little unreal, isn't it?" Tania said softly and Katy realized that she'd lapsed into silence.

"I knew about magic," Katy said honestly. "But I never knew it could be like this."

She was kind of dying to ask how it had gone for each of them. Had they gracefully accepted their fates right away or had they resisted their call? Had they been whisked away for a rags-to-riches Hallmark movie?

"It's pretty amazing," Carina volunteered, with her own foolish smile. "Weird, having all those extra feelings in your head, but...amazing."

"Am I really feeling what might be? From the future?"

She was met with nods, from all of them.

"All spells fade," Tania said. She had a southern American accent, and she spoke like she was reading poetry. "None of us have the magic sharing our emotions anymore, but the love that was predicted is real now."

"I kind of want to kill him sometimes, of course," Carina added merrily. "But in the very best and most loving way. And hoo, boy, does he light me on fire."

The laughter, which had been a mild, polite chuckle whenever something witty was said until then, took a genuine, relaxed tone. They all flushed and looked a little mortified that Carina had said something out loud, but even Leinani was grinning.

"Truth," Tania said. "Whatever else is involved in the

selection process of the spell, sexual compatibility isn't in question."

"Well, that's a relief," Katy said, not sure exactly how she'd gotten into a discussion this frank so fast with a handful of actual, factual princesses, but not exactly sorry that she had. "He sort of ran away instead of having a conversation, but I'd say that there was definitely...a spark."

"A spark, or a wildfire?" Leinani said slyly, her eyes dancing.

"Conversation is completely optional," Carina laughed.

"It's like a fairy tale," Mackenzie said quietly, smiling into her soda. "A happy ending I never expected."

"It *is* really best when the spell is strongest," Carina said knowingly. "Don't miss a chance to make the most of it. In bed, especially."

Tania chuckled. "She's crude, but not wrong! I was honestly sorry I waited so long."

Mackenzie was blushing and looked uncomfortable but pleased. "It's a sensible spell," she said. "It's easier to get past the awkward early phases of a relationship when you know what they're feeling, without having to guess or ask." She said it wistfully, and Katy remembered that she *hadn't* been able to sense Kenth's emotions when they met.

"It's not what I imagined a love spell would be," Katy confessed. "It's not unpleasant, and I could see how it might be...fun, but it's not what I expected."

"It's less heart-eyes and more *wow, where are all these **feels** coming from!*" Carina agreed.

"It's hard to sort them out," Leinani agreed mildly. "And it's hard to tell when the magic goes away, because you still have so many of your own at the end of it and you know him so well."

Katy might have asked more questions, burning with curiosity and loosened with exhaustion and gin and tonic,

THE DRAGON PRINCE'S MAGIC

but one of the uniformed guards popped her head in and announced that dinner was ready. Tania got stiffly up from her chair, waving off Mackenzie's unspoken offer for help, and the two of them left as Carina gathered up all of their glasses and took them to the bar before following them.

Katy found herself thinking about Raval, about the way she wanted to leave all her inhibitions on the floor and climb him like a tree. Mackenzie called it a sensible spell, but Katy felt anything but sensible. She felt swept away, like she was caught in a current of emotion and lust.

And it wasn't really a river that she wanted to swim against.

"Should I change before dinner?" Katy asked, hesitating at the door. Only Leinani remained, but she would know the protocols if anyone did.

"You're fine the way you are. It's very casual here," the princess assured her. Then she unexpectedly added, "Don't wait."

"To change?" Katy said it teasingly, though she wasn't entirely sure of the joke.

Leinani gave her the faintest of smiles and Katy knew she was being humored. "Don't wait with Raval. I know it probably seems a little fast and out of control, but the spell is fleeting and it's not something you want to miss. Enjoy it, while you have time, and know that being a princess isn't all ballgowns and tiaras. You don't know what's going to happen, but the spotlight you're going to find yourself in won't be entirely comfortable. Alaska has enemies!"

Crazy cult-leading enemies, apparently, on top of the garden-variety political tensions that Katy had come to the castle expecting. "More enemies than just Amara?"

"It would be very naïve to assume that anyone with power does not have enemies from many angles. Even if people don't know that the Small Kingdoms have actual dragon rulers, many know that the kingdoms are protected by a great deal of power, both supernatural and political. This alone makes them a target of envy."

Katy remembered with a jolt that Leinani herself was Small Kingdoms royalty. "Are you a…"

She nodded solemnly. "I am a dragon shifter."

Katy asked the first question that leapt to her mind. "Do you have a hoard?"

This smile was genuine, sparked by surprise. "I do, but you would find it rather modest," the princess said.

"Bottlecaps?" Katy guessed. "Pulp magazines? Those were the things I collected."

Leinani gave a warm laugh and looked sheepish. "Pokémon cards. Some of them are very rare and valuable."

"I'd love to see them sometime," Katy said. "I wrote some terrible fanfiction once, but I never had cards worth anything, and I gave them away ages ago."

To her surprise, Leinani went beet red, and she looked desperately towards the door. "Oh, here is Guard Tabor, wondering what is keeping us from dinner. I don't wish to leave everyone waiting." She hurried out without a backwards glance.

Katy followed bemusedly and wondered exactly what kind of fanfiction the prim Leinani had written.

CHAPTER 8

Raval concentrated hard on not dreading dinner with everyone, reminding himself that anything that he felt, Katy would, too. He didn't ever want to dampen a single ray of that woman's sunshine, and while the bond eased a tiny bit without immediate proximity, he could only imagine what his worries must feel like. They were unpleasant enough to himself.

Instead, he went to throw himself into the project of his heart. There was no puppy at the door to return to the kennel this time, and the garage was blissfully entirely his own.

It was the size of some sports fields, and it had high recessed windows that were dark most of the day at this time of year. There were a few limos near the entrance; these were the cars they used most.

Most of the brothers had a car of their choice. Fask's was a staid black BMW, and Kenth's Jeep was covered in a cloth because he had been gone so long the staff got tired of dusting it. Tray had a few sports cars. Toren had a highly impractical convertible that he rarely drove and Carina's beat-up white VW camper van looked out of place. She had let them give it a new coat of paint, but she insisted that the dents and stained trim were part of its charm.

Raval's project car was at the back, near his workroom.

It was a shining 1959 DeSoto Firedome wagon, mint green with a white racing stripe, and the hood was open. The last piece of the alternator (aftermarket, because the original parts had degraded too far) was lying out on his heavy wooden workbench.

Was it just coincidence that he was so close to finishing at last, on the same day that he'd met his mate? It just needed a few more days of concentration, a last, good push, and Raval wasn't sure what he would do with himself when it was done.

The summons to dinner was jarring, but Raval reluctantly put down the Dremel he'd been working with and washed up in the utility sink, humming with anxious anticipation, like an echo of the tool's vibration.

He would see Katy at dinner, and he both craved her presence and dreaded it. Was he going to make a fool of himself? Had Fask told the others yet?

Some of his questions were answered the moment he stepped into the formal dining hall. He expected prickly agitation and anxiety, but when he spotted Katy, everything seemed to fall into a perfect pattern of contentment.

She was sitting near the middle of the long table, the children lined up neatly past her, with an empty chair beside her. Raval didn't have to guess if he was meant to sit there because she spotted him and gave a brilliant smile and beckoning wave, and he could feel the anticipation and joy that the sight of him had brought her.

It was bizarre that he could do that, that *he* could cause a feeling of happy expectation.

"Nice of you to join us," Rian observed from across the

table as Raval took his seat. Did they think he *wouldn't* come? Was it a dig on the way he sometimes missed meals when he was working on a project, or did they think he'd be avoiding his mate because he wasn't particularly good with people?

"It's nice to see you," Katy said. "I'd take credit for saving you a seat, but your Mrs. James arranged everything."

"Then there were five," Toren intoned.

Well, that meant everyone knew, as if Raval's seat at her side wasn't obvious enough.

"Fask must be steaming," Drayger observed, *sotto voce*, down the table.

"Because he's a dragon?" one of the children wanted to know.

There was a little bubble of wonder from Katy; she wasn't used to the idea. "Let's use our table manners," she reminded them. "Which fork do I start with? Do I put my napkin on my head? Where do my elbows go?" A little girl yanked her elbows from the table at the reminder.

She laughingly let the kids demonstrate royal table manners, drawing Raval in with little sideways smiles.

Dinner was far less awful than he thought it would be, largely because Katy was the most amazing companion he could ever have imagined. She neatly deflected every uncomfortable scrutiny with a joke or a clever observation. She lobbed him easy conversational hooks and looked interested in his replies. She clearly already had a handle on the children, with a pitch-perfect sense of humor and a balance of tolerance and discipline that proved to Raval that her selection as live-in teacher had not *solely* been a quirk of the Compact's matchmaking.

The meal was actually pleasant, and Katy only tried to touch him once, aborting the motion at his flare of alarm when he saw her fingers about to land. She even made it look like she had simply fumbled her napkin as she avoided making contact at the last moment.

Raval left the dinner table as early as he could manage, while they were still teasing more information from Katy and talking about her plans with the kids.

Should he kiss her goodbye? He thought that maybe she would have liked that, but with everyone watching, what if he missed her mouth? He had a swirl of reservations that he wasn't sure were hers or his.

So Raval just left, and went to his room to lie on his bed staring up at the tall, arched ceiling reminding himself to blink at proper intervals because once he started thinking about things like that, sometimes he forgot how to do it subconsciously.

He wasn't sure how much time actually passed, but Raval knew that Katy was at his door even before she knocked.

He had no idea *why* she would be there, though. Courtesy dictated that he open the door for her, so he did, staring at her in consternation. "Why are you here?" he demanded, before he could think of a better way to ask.

Fortunately, Katy only smiled and laughed, glancing back at the guards shadowing her down the hall.

She laughed at everything, Raval thought with relief. She laughed when things were hard, and when they were easy, not just when they were funny. She must have felt some of his consternation and confusion through the mate bond, and she was trying to make him feel better.

"I'm here to have sex with you," she said frankly, her eyes still crinkled up in humor.

Raval was sure that he'd heard her wrong. What rhymed with sex? Was there a meal after dinner that he'd forgotten about? He did sometimes forget about meals. But she wasn't holding any food, just her purse.

"Can I come in?" she asked. "I mean, we could do it in the

hall, but the guards are out here, and I bet your bed would be more comfortable."

Raval was still standing in the way, because he still wasn't sure why she was there, and he went from *forgot to move* to *couldn't move* when she sidled up closer to him. She really *was* there to have sex with him, he could *feel* her excitement at the prospect.

It didn't feel anything at all like excitement for food.

"Why?" he blurted.

She was standing so close now that he could actually feel the heat of her, like she was a little furnace on a cold day. No, maybe that was attraction, his own heat for *her*.

"Because this isn't going to last forever," Katy said warmly. One of her hands was on his chest, and she was gently pushing him backwards into his room. She turned away to close the door behind her and toss her purse onto a nearby chair. "The princesses had a lot of helpful advice, and all of them agreed that it would be a real crime to miss an opportunity to make love to you while the mate bond is still strong."

Raval froze where she left him, still feeling the imprint of her hand on his chest through his shirt.

"I'm not sure..." he said.

Katy's eyes were the deepest brown he'd ever seen, dark and full of light at the same time. "I think you are," she said gently.

Then she was even closer, her whole body against his as her arms slipped up around his neck and Raval knew that she was right. He *was* sure. He was sure that this was exactly what he wanted. Every inch of him wanted to claim every inch of her. He needed the feel of her skin under his fingers, the springy touch of her hair, the heat and healing of her.

He lowered his face to hers, gauging his kiss to her response, and even he would not have needed the mate bond to know how much she liked it. Her mouth was alive under his, and her hands drew him closer as she whimpered in need. Her hips were moving in invitation against him, and one of his hands somehow found the curve of her waist and the slope of her ass.

Soaring beyond the physical was the song of the mate bond, showing him exactly how much she loved what he was doing, and how much she enjoyed knowing how much that *he* loved it, too. It was a spiral of pleasure so intense that Raval was dizzy. He didn't have to guess where his hands should go, he could feel where she liked his touch best, and he had no idea how much time passed before they moved from casually making out with clothing on to unbuttoning each other with fingers that trembled with excitement.

"Bed," he said desperately. "I have a bed."

"I thought you might," she answered.

CHAPTER 9

Katy had not actually gone to Raval's rooms with the intention of sleeping with him. She had planned to have an actual conversation, see what their common ground was, and put their relationship into perspective. She'd braced herself for finding a physical relationship challenging, or for being rebuffed altogether.

First of all, they had only just met that morning. Katy wasn't the type to take it slow, but she was also not usually a same-day-sex kind of girl. Especially knowing how much scrutiny she was under. The other princesses had certainly implied that no one else was expecting her to wait very long, but Katy wondered if *that very night* wasn't pushing things a little.

She also knew—both from observation and internet speculation—that Raval wasn't entirely neurotypical, and sometimes that came with hypersensitivity to touch. She watched his brothers give him extra space, though they probably didn't even realize they were doing it—it looked like an ingrained habit.

And when she accidentally nearly brushed his arm at

dinner, it had raised a spike of panic in him that Katy wanted to immediately soothe.

That could mean he disliked touch altogether, and that sex might be overwhelming and uncomfortable for him. She was ready to work through it with him, prepared for patience and temperance so that they could find a good balance of what they both wanted. They might need the full duration of the mate bond, she told herself. It was *practical* to approach their physical relationship sooner than later, not just that she was absolutely *desperate*.

But when he opened the door, she knew to her bones that he wanted her just as badly as she wanted him, and she couldn't think of a reason not to cut to the chase.

And once he let himself touch her, he was *all in*.

Katy definitely wanted him *all in*.

She almost asked if he was a virgin, then decided it didn't matter. What mattered was getting him out of his shirt, of pulling that crisp fabric off of his broad, fit shoulders and finding that his chest was even more perfect than she'd imagined, barely covered in a downy layer of fuzz as blond as the hair on his head.

Whether he was a virgin or not, he was definitely not experienced in undressing another person and Katy had to keep herself from stripping herself in the interest of efficiency. She was rewarded by the awe and honor in his hands as he uncovered every inch of skin and worshiped it like it was an accomplishment.

His mouth was uncertain at first and gradually more confident. Every trailing finger was intense, every kiss was hotter than the last, and when there was no clothing between them and he was pressing into her, Katy wasn't sure which of them was more hungry for that carnal contact.

She could feel his pleasure, the coiling spiral of his building pressure, inside of her, in her head and filling her

THE DRAGON PRINCE'S MAGIC

core. It took only the barest of direction—*here, yes! more!*—and he was pressing her down on his bed, every inch of his skin electric against hers.

His cock was exactly as perfect as the rest of him, and Katy felt like she'd won some kind of Nanny-Prince lottery when it slipped into her waiting, wanting lips. She was a tangle of begging—*more-now!*—and trying to slow down and savor every slow, sizzling stroke as he filled her.

They moved together absolutely perfectly, like bars of music, or like the strokes of paint in a masterpiece.

He didn't run her over in his need, raising her to ecstatic heights and then waiting for her fall, not once but twice before he let himself do the same, and she felt his stunning release, almost as strongly as she felt her own.

He cradled her afterwards, and Katy could feel his deep contentment as well as the slowing hammer of his heart.

"Tell me about magic," she said softly, tracing patterns along his arms. He had the most *magnificent* muscles. "And I don't mean the kind we just made." She thought about the echo of his pleasure in hers. "Well, maybe that kind, too."

"You know a little about it?" Raval guessed.

"Spells have to be written, they're labor-intensive and full of catches. Lots of people who know about them want to be casters, not many can. It's generally much easier and faster to do things the mundane way."

"It takes a lot of concentration, a lot of hard focus, a lot of time," Raval agreed, nodding. Katy was particularly glad that he enjoyed skin contact as much as she did. His body was absolutely delicious against hers, even as sated as she felt now, and she could feel his hum of joyful afterglow, too. They spooned absolutely perfectly, the entire length of their bodies pressed together.

Katy felt like he was writing magic on her now, his hand making lazy patterns on her belly.

"All magic fades," Raval said thoughtfully, and Katy felt an undercurrent of worry and concern to him.

She had a pang of regret to think that they might not have this beautiful magical connection forever. But the other mates had said that they had bonds that were, if anything, even stronger now. This was a gift for now, a tantalizing glimpse of their future, to be replaced with a genuine love that would grow between them.

Whatever else Katy felt about free will and destiny, she thought that she could do a lot worse than loving Raval. Even putting aside the fact that he was a hunky prince who lived in a beautiful castle and could allegedly change into a dragon, Katy was beginning to realize that there was a depth of emotion and intelligence to this man that appealed to something at her very core. He seemed serious and Katy guessed that he would be very opaque to someone who didn't have a direct line to the complex and compelling person beneath his cool facade. He was smart, clever, and kind, though Katy thought that he might not agree to any of her assessments.

"Tell me about your spells," Katy invited.

She could feel him get shy in her head, but he bravely said, "I've been working on a project for a long time that I should be able to show you in just a few days. All the components are done, all I have to do is reassemble it, now."

"I can't wait to see it," Katy said genuinely. "What does it do?"

"I'm not sure."

From anyone else, Katy might have suspected a joke, but she could feel Raval's seriousness. "How long have you been working on it?"

"Thirteen years."

"That's a long time to work on something when you don't know what it will do," Katy said with a giggle that she hoped sounded kind. Then she remembered that Raval would be able to tell that she meant it warmly. This was the best kind of magic, she thought contentedly. But she could also tell that Raval was a little chagrined about his mysterious project, and the last thing she wanted to do was make him feel bad, so she changed the subject.

They talked long into the night, Katy teasing details about his childhood out of him and sharing stories of her own. They compared tastes in music (compatible), media (sorely divergent), and bad habits.

"I get excited and talk with my mouth full," she confessed. "And I can't keep a secret to save my life. What about you?"

"I take jokes too literally," Raval said seriously.

"Do they go over your head, or are you too tall for that?" Katy teased.

That did make him chuckle and squeeze her close. "Don't expect me to be funny like you," he warned. "I'll gnaw on a punchline for a week."

"Don't worry," Katy said warmly. "I can be funny enough for both of us."

"I'll try to remember to laugh," Raval promised. "But you can do the humor for both of us."

There *was* an *us*, she thought, squirming around in his arms to kiss him. There was an *us* and it was absolutely breathtaking. She was in a fantasy fairy tale, lying in thousand-count cotton sheets with a possibly-dragon-shifting prince with arms like an athlete, all of their future possible love humming in her veins.

She vowed to savor every moment of this unexpected enchantment, to live each second of it to the fullest. She would have to get up ridiculously early, but it was worth losing a little sleep to enjoy a little more of this magic.

And he was already kissing her back, showing with his body that he too was interested in living to the *fullest*...

CHAPTER 10

Raval remained awake after Katy drifted happily off to sleep and he hoped that the rush of misgivings he could feel when she was quiet in his head would not disturb her rest or color her dreams.

It was so easy to think that everything was going to be perfect when she was awake, her relentless optimism and bubbly joy making his head feel like a symphony or a meadow full of flowers on a sunny summer day.

His mind had never been such a pleasant place to be, and Raval desperately hoped that his own thoughts weren't dragging her down as much as she was lifting him up.

It wouldn't last, he reminded himself. Spells always had a limited duration. Even Mackenzie's wild chaos magic faded quickly. He tried to figure how long the bond might last, based on everything his brothers had described. He needed a calendar and more data—they were always frustratingly imprecise, he'd have to ask them for more details.

For now, he could tell what she was feeling, and she could *understand* him. Raval had to pause and suck in his breath at the unexpected pleasure of the idea of it. He hadn't realized how starved he was for someone else to comprehend him. He'd gone through life feeling half out of step with everything. Oh, he could fake his way through most social interactions, just by studying what other people did and trying to emulate them the best he could. His dragon was of great assistance, hissing in his ear to remind him of basic etiquette, but he'd never found it natural and easy the way that others did, and he had craved someone to see him through that facade and…still like him.

And Katy *did* like him.

It wasn't just attraction, though Raval could dispassionately see that desire played a significant role in how well they'd hit it off. But he could also tell that she *liked* him, that she got *happier* when she saw him, that she *enjoyed* being around him. She seemed to think that he was a fun puzzle, not just an off-putting cipher, and he liked her style of asking questions.

Around most people, he felt all wound up, like he had to pretend to be something he wasn't, like he couldn't relax or be himself. But with Katy, he had nothing left to hide, and it somehow didn't leave him ashamed or out of step.

He felt like he was home with her.

And he had to treasure every moment of it, because he knew that it was fleeting and when it was gone…

Raval balked at the idea.

As soon as the spell faded, he'd be back to himself, clueless and opaque to basic social cues that everyone else found so simple. He wouldn't know when to touch her, or how to make her happy. His brothers might have good advice, but he didn't even know the questions to ask.

CHAPTER 11

A long habit of rising early got Katy reluctantly from Raval's embrace in the morning, lingering over kisses and caresses until she could untangle herself from his sexy long legs and sleepy sighs.

The same guards were still stoically waiting by the door and Katy thought she finally understood the term *walk of shame*, keenly aware of her disheveled state as she slipped out of Raval's rooms. She lifted her chin and met their eyes—and found only amusement and approval, which she answered with an embarrassed laugh as she scampered back to her rooms for a lightning-fast shower.

The day was busy with teaching and playing with the children of the castle, working hard to prove that she wasn't slacking on her duties just because she'd been unexpectedly attached to one of the princes. No one said a word of judgment about the bed she hadn't slept in, and she focused all of her energy on her students.

She threw out the curriculum she'd planned wholesale, awed by what she found in their assessment workbooks. They were breathtakingly honest, absolutely unafraid to try things and take chances, and if they had some shocking gaps in their knowledge, they also had a firm grip on rational thought and spacial thinking.

Before she tackled any school topics, she set them to the job of showing her around the castle, to show her their favorite places, and teach *her* the rules. She was pleased and delighted that they stepped up to the challenge. Franky took the class to the kitchen and somberly explained to Katy which snacks they were permitted to help themselves to. Danny took her to the portrait gallery. Jin took them out to the dog yard.

The staff clearly adored the children. Nathaniel, in the dog yard, hooked up a team and took them all out on sled runs. In the kitchen, they were slipped cookies and carrots. Fask even let them into the throne room, where they took turns sitting on the carved seats. Katy was thrilled that they had the capacity to play at make-believe, given everything that they'd been through.

She had feared from their quiet obedience that they were truly broken in spirit, but they were quickly warming up and trusting her, and it was clear that they were all very bright and creative.

Randal took them to the library. As Mackenzie had advised her, the way to the quiet boy's heart was through history and Katy was happy to explore the library with him selecting an armful of books to read.

If the rest of the castle was in places very Alaska-practical, with a lot of dog-friendly vinyl installed instead of slippery tile or cold stone, and a modern kitchen with a monster of a modern dishwasher, the library was an appropriately decadent fairy tale treasure hoard.

Besides a full bar and a comfortable reading and socialization nook, it had a big fireplace, and giant bay windows with thick velvet curtains. She was pretty sure there was a secret passageway somewhere, if she went looking for one. It just had that kind of aesthetic.

"This collection was started by the first king of Alaska, Ladranyikayer," Tania said, showing them around. "Some of these books are very rare." If she was leery about handing expensive books over to a reserved teenage boy, she didn't show it, and she was happy to explain the filing system so they could find more.

Randal was particularly interested in Alaskan history and devoured three of the early volumes in a single afternoon.

"Is he retaining much of it?" Katy asked Mackenzie in an aside as the other kids worked on a scavenger hunt she had set up for them. To her surprise, they had completely bypassed the competitive nature she had intended for the exercise and had turned it into a collaboration instead. They were currently searching the castle for a key and a sprig of lavender that she had planted in the kitchen earlier. "He reads exceptionally fast."

"His recall isn't quite eidetic," Mackenzie said, "but it's good. He'll memorize the facts that interest him the most. You'll have trouble getting him to do anything in any other subject, I'm afraid."

"I've had kids like this before," Katy said. "All you have to do is come at it from an angle they love. Instead of math, we'll study math history. Instead of the rules of science, we focus on how the discoveries were made in the past by important people and talk about the ones in Alaska, particularly. He'll still absorb the important bits, but approaching the subject from an area he feels confident in will help it not seem intimidating. I can squeeze a lot of the basics in around the edges without putting a lot of emphasis on them."

Mackenzie looked at her in wonder. "That would probably work with him."

Katy made a show of rubbing her nails on her shirt and

appraising them in pride, but Mackenzie only looked puzzled at the gesture.

She was not honestly sure how well she'd have been able to manage the children without Mackenzie's assistance. It wasn't that they were ever disobedient or acted out, but they were completely clueless about modern slang, popular media, and conveniences that Katy had never thought twice about. Mackenzie was invaluable in helping when Katy wasn't sure if there was a language barrier or just a lack of common ground. She had to go through some things that were laughably basic and there were other things that they handled far beyond their age level.

She suspected that Mackenzie was correct about their true age being older than their physical bodies, and wished she had some way to truth it other than their unexpected maturity.

They were also very insular. They knew and trusted each other, working in a collective tandem that Katy had never witnessed outside of very close siblings.

She wondered how they would ever cope with being broken up and placed in individual families. She could not imagine that it would be an easy transition for them.

And all day, her thoughts returned inevitably to Raval.

It wasn't just to the acrobatic sex that they'd had or the long night of erotic cuddling, though certainly her body was still tingling with satisfaction and renewed longing. Most of all, Katy remembered the triumph of making him laugh, and the joy of lying together just talking. He was like the other half that she hadn't realized that she was missing.

She'd been warned as part of the hiring process that she wouldn't be able to maintain private contact with her family as a matter of security, but she wished that she could text her sister Emaline right now. There weren't enough eggplant emojis in the world to send, and what a laugh they would

THE DRAGON PRINCE'S MAGIC

have together over the fact that she'd slept with one of the princes on her very first night in the castle.

She and Raval had only a few moments alone together during that entire day, stolen after lunch while Mrs. James and Mackenzie took the kids to be fitted for more clothing.

"Will you be…ah…available later?" he wanted to know. Her guards were discretely distant, though Katy knew that they were just at the end of the hall. How far did sound carry in a castle?

"I should be able to come see you after I see the kids to bed," she said, trying to sound cool about it. Just planning a hot tryst with a prince. No big deal.

"I'd like that," Raval said quietly.

Katy was honestly surprised that the air between them wasn't warped with heat. She could feel how much he wanted her, and she was a ridiculous wanton knot of desire herself. She kept picturing his broad bare shoulders, and the way his stomach sucked in when she dragged fingernails along his side, and further down where—

Raval cleared his throat. "Later, then!" he said abruptly.

Anyone watching them would have thought he was angry with her, but Katy knew better.

She didn't have time for the cold shower she desperately needed, so she dived into distracting herself with work. Curiously, she could feel Raval doing the same, concentrating all of his attention on something compelling.

CHAPTER 12

Raval knew exactly what to do with Katy the second night she came to his door, and he didn't waste time or words. He flung open the door and slammed it shut again behind her so hard that it bounced open. Kissing her up against it closed it again, and Katy was alive in his arms and under his skin.

They made love urgently, more roughly than Raval would ever have dared if he wasn't sure of how much she liked it when he held her wrists against the door and dragged his teeth along her neck.

He was pretty sure that he tore her shirt, getting her out of it, and didn't care that he lost a button on his pants. They wanted each other like he'd never dared to want anything in his life and she was so cool and healing in his head. He wanted to crawl inside her and live there forever, to be closer than flesh could even allow, and the only thing that soothed his urges was the sweet velvet of her skin and the heat of her as he entered her at last.

They didn't make it to the bed, only to the rug before the

fireplace in his sitting room. He had one fleeting moment to wish he'd made a fire, and then it didn't matter any more.

He gentled his strokes because it matched her desire and they moved together like music through a half dozen time signatures and positions that Raval had never considered. He hadn't realized the many ways that bodies could fit together, and now he wanted to try them *all.*

They took each other to plateaus of pleasure and then lay together at last while Raval tried to gather all the scattered pieces of his brain again in the aftermath.

He should tell her, he thought. He should get in the habit of saying things out loud, in anticipation of the time when she wouldn't understand him inside.

"Good. That. Good. Was. That was good." That was considerably less impressive than he'd hoped.

She won't care if you are inarticulate, his dragon assured him, as content and sated as Raval and Katy were.

But she did, because she could sense the effort it had taken him, and she propped up on one elbow and smiled down at him in encouragement. "That *was* good," she agreed without teasing him. "That was *delicious.*"

They kissed slowly, and Raval enjoyed the taste of her no less for having satisfied his body's baser urges.

"A shower?" he suggested.

"You could talk me into that," Katy agreed, getting to her feet and offering him a hand. Raval accepted the hand but used his own power to rise, resisting his urge to pull her back down with him.

Most bathrooms echoed miserably, and were too bright and forceful, so Raval had designed his as a tactile haven. It was finished in smooth, dark stone, with recessed lights on brightness control that he kept low. Thick absorbent throw rugs on the floor muffled the sound and soothed his bare feet, and he could step off onto cool, hard tile between them if he needed that kind of grounding. The shower alcove was big enough to spread his arms out in, so he never felt confined in it, and one wall was natural stone. The multiple rain heads were each adjustable, from needle-hard to the barest patter, and Raval had tinkered with the temperature control until it ranged from summer-rain cool to blistering hot, each head independent.

"What a shower! Is that a spell?" Katy asked, stepping into it and tracing her fingers over the words he'd laboriously carved along the wall. She was gloriously, distractingly naked, her brown-skinned body a mesmerizing collection of curves. "Oh, you're embarrassed!" She said, even before Raval had recognized it himself.

"Why does this embarrass you?" she wanted to know, turning to quiz him.

"It's selfish," Raval said, knowing that he couldn't deny anything she felt.

"Selfish?" Katy tilted her head, trying to follow the letters around the organic planes of the rocks. "What does it do?"

"I'll show you."

Raval turned on the water in the usual way, with the aged-copper faucet handle that pierced the stone wall. There was a brief hiss and the shower heads began to stream steaming hot water. He kept the temperature lower than he could stand, not wanting to scald her.

Katy tipped her head up and let the water run over her face. "Oh, that's glorious!" she said. "Is it magic?"

"No, but this is..." Raval dragged his fingers over a well-worn passage. "Pause," he said.

All of the water stopped, every particle still suspended in midair, and Katy sucked in her breath.

Every drop was a motionless jewel, and they were standing in a chamber of glistening enchantment. It was beautiful, which had not been part of Raval's original purpose, but he was glad of it now, because Katy loved it so much.

"I've never seen anything like it," she gasped. "I'm in a *chandelier!*"

She swept a hand through the hanging drops, dragging them along behind her in a trail of sparkling lights.

"I was going to change the light color, too," Raval admitted. "But that was a lot easier to do with adjustable LEDs than with a spell." He demonstrated the switch, changing the color from white to a cool blue and setting it to rotate randomly across the spectrum. He'd set it to change slowly, so it wasn't jarring.

Katy made a squeal of delight like a tea kettle. "This is the most amazing thing I've ever seen in my life." She continued to make swirls of disturbance in the droplets, breaking them into tinier slivers of light. "You *are* magic," she said in awe. Then she scrutinized him. "Why does this make you feel *guilty?*"

"It's frivolous," Raval said frankly. "It serves no one but me. It was months of work that I did only for myself. It can't be duplicated and I don't even want anyone in my bathroom to enjoy it." He quickly added, "Except for you."

"You're allowed to have projects for yourself," Katy said kindly.

Raval could not feel a single hint of any disappointment in her, so she must not understand. "It was a lot of work. I ought to focus that kind of effort on something that betters humanity or saves lives or fixes realistic problems."

There was a softness to Katy's mind that made Raval recognize all the prickles of his own.

"I love you," she said. "I love you to the very bottom of your giant heart." Everything was absolutely perfect for a moment when she stood up on her tiptoes to kiss him, putting one hand along his jaw.

But all spells fade and the water began to slowly slide downward again, gathering speed over a few moments until it was falling normally again. The kiss was over, and she was laughing and investigating his options of soap.

Would her love also fade like magic, and wash away so swiftly?

CHAPTER 13

The second morning she left Raval's room, Katy exchanged casual waves with the guards and nearly fell over when her half-fastened shoe slipped off. She felt like maybe she wasn't so much in a royal nanny romance novel as she was in an over-the-top comedy. The Nanny Next Door, maybe. Or The Prince's Naughty Nanny. Maybe The Prince's Governess Gives Head.

The feeling of him humming in her brain buoyed her through a day more challenging than the two previous; the children were clearly feeling bold enough to start testing their boundaries. Katy was honestly glad to see it, and she encouraged their mild pranks and established guidelines that they respected without question or protest. Raval retreated to his mysterious project, and they were both too busy to see each other until late into the night.

The third morning, however, there wasn't a shred of amusement or approval when the very same guards met her at the door, carrying their weapons.

"Captain Luke needs to see you," one of them said grimly.

"Right now," the other added.

Katy gave a squeak. She was wearing the clothing she'd put on the day before, and had been looking forward to a quick shower before the lessons for the day started. She'd opted not to put her bra on for the short trip down the hall, and was holding it awkwardly in one hand. She tried not to draw attention to it, wondering if she could get it unobtrusively into one of her wholly unworthy pockets, or better yet, her purse, but that only made the shorter of the two guards brandish his gun. "Let's see your hands."

Katy lifted the offending garment. "It's a bra. Industrial strength, because there's a lot of me, but not really weapon-worthy." Not against *guns* or the carved magic-looking spears.

"What's going on?" Raval asked from behind her, and Katy had a rush of gratitude that was her own and a wave of worry that wasn't. Her alarm at the guards' greeting must have woken him up the rest of the way. "What do you want with her?"

How could just his presence make her feel so much better? It wasn't like Katy expected him to be able to protect her from bullets, if the guards chose to shoot, but she wasn't afraid of them any more.

"We're not at liberty to say," the first guard said officiously, but when Raval stepped forward with a growl, the second swiftly added, "Captain Luke just said to bring her right away. The kids are gone."

All of Katy's mortification at her unplanned bra display dissolved into panic and alarm. "They're gone?" She didn't wait for the guards to keep up with her, bolting down the hallway for the school room. There were more guards around the corner, but Katy completely ignored them and plowed into the room. "Are all of them *gone?*"

Prince Kenth was standing in the center of the room,

clutching a wailing Dalaya. "Not all of them," he snarled at Katy.

Mackenzie was weeping, circling the room and wringing her hands. "What do I do?" she cried. "How did it happen?" The air seemed to crackle around her.

Fask was shouting about security, and Captain Luke was barking orders into a phone, calling for a lockdown of the castle, the immediate account of every member of the guard and the staff, and possibly a beheading; Katy was having trouble tracking all the conversations happening at once.

Kenth was futilely trying to calm both Dalaya and Mackenzie, but even Katy could see that he was at a breaking point himself. There was no sign of struggle, but there was a singed circle in the carpet in the center of the room, and Cindy's beloved stuffed rabbit was lying just outside of it. Two of the other brothers were pacing the perimeter, and Tania was standing in the doorway, dressed in a silky loose dressing gown with her mouth in a little O of horror. Leinani was standing beside her, dressed for the outdoors. Fask was trying to talk to Captain Luke, and the princes were asking loud questions.

But one thing was obvious. The children, aside from Dalaya, were gone. Katy went to their bunkroom. Their beds all looked freshly slept in, and the curtains over the windows were still drawn. Their slippers were lined up neatly beside their bunks, exactly as she'd seen them when she and Mrs. James had tucked them in the night before.

"Get back! Don't touch me! I don't know what I will do!" Mackenzie looked like she was going to burst into flames, and Kenth was clearly juggling his distressed daughter against his desire to comfort and contain her. Katy stepped forward, finally recognizing a way that she could help and offered her arms for Dalaya.

"What's that?" Kenth wanted to know, looking at the bra she'd folded into an unrecognizable shape in one hand.

"My bra," Katy told him, mortified. "I was..."

It didn't really matter, at the moment, and Kenth dismissed whatever explanation Katy was grasping for to thrust Dalaya at her so that he could turn his attention to Mackenzie. "I know, love, I know," he said between gritted teeth. "Keep it in, you have to focus. You have to think. Don't let it get away with you."

Chaos magic, Katy remembered. She'd teased more information out of Carina the day before. Mackenzie's magic was unpredictable. Without the structure of spell magic, she might intend to retrieve the children but accidentally make a crater where the Alaskan castle had been.

Dalaya gave a single squawk of protest at her transference, then decided that Katy was safe, clinging to her like a multi-legged burr. Katy stepped back out of range of whatever it was that Mackenzie was going to do as Kenth drew her into his arms.

"I have to do something," Mackenzie was saying, her voice full of grief and anger. "What? What can I do? How do I get them back? I won't let her have them!"

"We'll figure something out," Kenth assured her. "Let's start with finding them," he suggested. "If we know where she took them..." he cast a look at Leinani. "Your ring?"

She shook her head regretfully. "I already tried. It didn't respond. Amara has probably neutralized it."

Captain Luke was hanging up her phone and glaring at the screen, and the guards and brothers and mates were all milling around.

"We need to stay calm," Fask was saying, sounding not the slightest bit calm.

"I have an idea."

It wasn't the voice that any of them was expecting, and

Katy could feel Raval's alarm and discomfort when everyone turned to regard him.

He blinked and looked at Katy like he was throwing her a rope to haul him back with. She willed him confidence. "I have a car," he said, and she remembered the car that he'd been building for thirteen years. "We might be able to get them back with it. But I need Mackenzie."

"How will a car help?" Mackenzie demanded. "I don't know how to drive."

"It's doubtful that Amara portaled the kids to a place within driving distance," Carina said, like she was trying to lighten the mood but failing.

Raval's brothers, however, were looking at him thoughtfully.

"Are we finally going to find out what that thing does?" Toren said.

But Raval had said that he didn't know what it did, either.

He didn't answer, only turned and left. Katy paused only a moment before dashing to follow him, Dalaya still clinging to her neck.

CHAPTER 14

Raval was keenly aware of the trail of people behind him on the trek to the garage, like an ill-planned parade with no spectators. Katy was closest at his heels, and she gasped and shivered at the cold, clasping Dalaya close to her.

He probably ought to put an arm around her to keep her warm or offer her a coat, but it wasn't far to the garage, and by the time he thought of it, they were there, stomping snow off their feet.

It was a quiet, cheerless group, and Raval felt like the quietest and most cheerless of all. He led them back to where the car waited. It was a big, boxy station wagon from the fifties, ungraceful next to his brothers' modern cars, and terribly dated with its mint green and chrome finish. The dashboard was fake wood paneling.

"Is it a car, or a boat?" Toren joked, but the effort at humor fell flat.

"What does it do?" Fask asked briskly. "How can it help us?"

"I made it to fix things," Raval said. "I started it when Mother died."

The mood in the garage went from uncertain to downright uncomfortable. Raval braced himself for an unwelcome wave of pity from Katy, but it was less jarring than he'd feared, and more gentle.

He was riddled with doubt. What if it didn't work? What if it wasn't helpful?

His dragon was pragmatic. *It is ready at last.* But he didn't know how it worked any more than Raval did.

"I don't understand how this can help," Mackenzie said, tracing her finger over some of the writing on the air intake. "I wish I could still read spells. This is incredibly complicated."

Tania was leaning over the open engine, her head cocked to one side as she followed the lines of letters that snaked over every metal component. There was even lettering on the rubber belts; those would be the parts of the spell with the least longevity, but they should work for a few uses at least. "How long did this *take* you?"

Dalaya fussed in Katy's arms and Kenth took her back.

"I've been working on it for thirteen years," Raval said. "And I finished it yesterday. But it won't work without Mackenzie."

Mackenzie blinked at him. "What do you need me for? This is structured magic."

"I'm pretty sure it breaks the rules of structured magic," Raval told her. "No one would ever be able to activate it. But *you* don't have to follow the rules."

"It portals," Tania guessed, peering sideways at the letters running down the inside of the alternator. "But it doesn't need an anchor."

"You left the destination up to the spell itself?" Mackenzie said incredulously. "That's desperately risky."

"I thought it might be a loophole," Raval said. "It should take you to where you need to be to *fix* it. Whatever *it* is."

"A loophole, maybe, but a terribly dangerous one. It's so vague." Mackenzie was shaking her head. "And you think I can...jumpstart it? And it will find the kids?" She must have sounded distressed, because Kenth was reaching for her and giving her shoulders a reassuring squeeze.

Raval knew the powerful pain of hope and he thought he recognized it in her now. "I don't know," he cautioned. "But it could."

"Let's try it," Mackenzie said at once, flexing her fingers.

"No." Of course Fask would have reservations. "We don't know what it will do. Raval, you're a fine caster…"

Fask always tried to start with a compliment when he was going to tell someone that they were wrong.

"We'll do it!" Raval wasn't sure if Kenth was siding with Mackenzie because she was his mate, if he actually thought that Raval's car would work, or if he just wanted to poke a finger in Fask's eye. "We haven't got a better choice right now, and the longer we wait, the more likely that we'll lose the trail."

Raval was afraid that this was going to precipitate a fight between the oldest brothers, but Tania was nodding approvingly and Toren was already peering into the driver's seat. "Where are the keys? Who's going?"

"I'm going," Mackenzie said at once.

"I am," Kenth growled. Dalaya was handed back to Katy, and Raval had to shunt away her nervousness and guilt. She felt responsible for the kids, and that was catalyst enough for Raval to reveal his car and do anything in his power to get them back.

Toren had opened the driver's door and Raval had to bite back his instinct to tell him to stop touching things. "We've got to leave room for all the kids, but this thing is cavernous, that shouldn't be a problem. You can probably squeeze them all in the hatchback if they're friendly. I'll go!"

"I'm no good in a fight," Carina said helplessly. "Don't do anything dumb without me."

"I'll go," Tray offered, and Leinani promptly echoed him.

"Raval, you should go, since you're the only one who understands this thing." Rian was frowning at the car. "We might fit four across in that back seat."

He exchanged a look with Fask, whose stewing was obvious even to Raval.

"Someone has to stay here and protect the palace," Fask said. "It could be a diversion." But he didn't try to stop them.

There were several quick kisses and embraces and Kenth and Mackenzie both gave a tearful Dalaya big hugs and then handed her back to Katy. Raval didn't remember that he ought to kiss Katy goodbye until she had her arms full of clingy, crying five-year-old. He dipped to give her the swiftest peck he could manage and between Katy's surprise and Dalaya's flailing, all he got was punched in the mouth with a tiny fist.

"Sorry!" Katy said.

"Sowwy!" Dalaya sobbed into her collar.

It was distinctly uncomfortable piling into the car, all of them shoulder-to-shoulder on the bench seats. It was a roomy car, but none of them were *small*. Mackenzie sat behind the wheel and Raval sat next to her, showing her what the parts of the car were - the gearshift, the ignition, the brake and gas and clutch. "You shouldn't have to actually drive it," Raval said, dreading what she might do to it.

"Aren't there seatbelts?" Toren was wedged in between Rian and Leinani. "Sorry, your highness. I'm not trying to be fresh."

Kenth reached across Raval to squeeze Mackenzie's

shoulder and she drew a shaky breath. "Let's do this," she said bravely.

She turned the key and to Raval's relief, the engine turned over with barely a stutter. "How does it activate?"

Raval drew in a breath and said out loud, "*I have to fix it.*" As magical incantations went, it wasn't terribly graceful, but it had been the litany on his mind as he first threw himself into the project.

Nothing happened. The engine continued to purr and tick, but they were still in the garage.

"Maybe you have to say it," Raval guessed. He'd always envisioned *himself* in the driver's seat.

"*I have to fix it!*" Mackenzie declared, loud near Raval's ear.

More nothing happened.

Mackenzie put both of her hands flat on the steering wheel and bowed her head, concentrating hard. The air around her got hot and charged, but the car continued to putter in place, and nothing outside them changed.

"Maybe we should get out and push?" Toren suggested. "Ouch!"

Tray had probably pinched him. "Give her a chance," he said mildly.

"You can do it," Leinani encouraged.

"*I have to fix it!*" Mackenzie said again.

Raval thought it sounded ridiculous, repeated, and wished he'd thought to use something more elegant. Latin, maybe. He was also finding it very awkward to be sitting between Kenth and Mackenzie.

Mackenzie tried a series of things, and they switched places, to Raval's relief, so that he could try it himself.

"Are we going to poison ourselves by running the car in the garage?" Toren wanted to know.

"The air handler should take care of it," Raval said shortly. His own attempts to get the car to go failed as well.

"Does it have to be driving?" Kenth suggested.

Raval pulled it out of the garage and drove the driveway loop, feeling supremely foolish as everything they tried failed, over and over again.

"Does Mackenzie have to drive it?" Toren theorized.

They let her try, at a straight stretch of driveway, and Raval winced over her grinding of the gears and their jerky progress. Twice, they went up on the icy walkway and Raval wished he had winter tires on.

"This isn't working!" she finally wept, slamming on the brakes.

Kenth crawled over Raval to take her into his arms and comfort her and Raval put on the parking brake before they could roll into the statue of their father.

"We'll figure something out," Kenth promised, rocking Mackenzie. "We'll get them back."

Everyone piled out of the car at the castle entrance and Raval drove it back to the garage alone, feeling hollow and defeated.

It was empty again, and echoing quiet when he slid the car into its space and turned it off.

He stared at the lettering on the steering wheel. Years of work. So much time and concentration and focus.

Were his intentions unclear? Had he lost track of something along the way? Was he a failure? This was supposed to be his masterpiece, his life's work.

A scrabbling sound caught his attention, and Raval turned to find that Lancelot was trotting in through the open garage door behind him, trailing his leash.

Raval sighed and opened the driver's door. "Dammit."

Lancelot was not interested in being carried again, and dashed behind one of his brother's cars when Raval went to catch him. Raval closed the garage door so that he couldn't escape again, and when he turned back, found that the puppy had climbed in through the open driver's door of the Firedome and was panting happily at him through the window.

"Hey, hon."

Raval would have noticed Katy's approach if he hadn't been so distracted by Lancelot's antics and his own frustrations.

She didn't try to touch him or comfort him, and Raval was glad of it. "I like your car," was all she said. "Mint green is one of my favorite colors."

"It was my mother's favorite color," Raval said. He'd bought it to fix up for her before she died.

"Oh, it's a puppy!" Katy opened the passenger door just enough to slip in and put her purse on the floor, and Lancelot promptly crawled into her lap and started licking her, whining and wiggling his entire body. "Oh my gosh, you are the cutest thing I've ever seen in my life. Look at your ears! Oh, your little teeth! Does my finger taste good? Gentle!"

Raval wasn't sure what else to do, so he went around to the other side of the car and slid into the driver's seat, closing the door to keep the dog trapped in with them.

"Where are you taking us?" Katy asked merrily.

"Taking us?" Raval didn't understand the joke, if it was one.

"Well, I'm pretty sure I just got fired for losing eleven children on my third day of work, but we've got this nice car and this very friendly dog, so maybe we should go on a road trip?"

She *was* joking, Raval was sure now. He guessed that it was a coping method, and he figured that as a coping method it certainly wasn't the worst one he'd ever witnessed. Probably, obsessing over a car for thirteen years was a lot less healthy.

"Tell me about it?" Katy invited.

"The road trip?"

"The road trip. Making the car. The puppy." Lancelot was squirming joyously in her arms and gnawing gently on her hand. She didn't seem to mind it. "Whatever you want to tell me."

Raval started at the end. "The puppy is Lancelot, one of Tray's puppies. He is an escape artist who has decided that the garage is an awesome place to hide. He's already chewed up two power cables. The car is a '59 DeSoto Firedome wagon. I bought it to restore for my mom...and then she died."

The sound of Lancelot worrying at Katy's fingers was the only sound for a moment. "What happened to her?" she finally asked.

Raval suspected that she was asking in order to make him open up about it, not because she hadn't heard the story.

"It was breakup," Raval said distantly. "When the river breaks up in the spring and she got washed away in a flash flood after an ice jam."

Lancelot's antics and wagging tail seemed very out of place and distracting in the car. It was weird, having anyone other than him in the Firedome, though it was better than having his brothers crammed in with him. It was especially weird having her sympathy in his head and...not minding it.

"I'm sorry," she said gently, because that was what people said about tragic stories like that. "You must have missed her a lot."

"Kenth blames himself," Raval observed dispassionately. "He was supposed to be helping with cleanup at a summer camp we had by the river, but Mom was doing it herself at the time. We've never been sure why she was so close to the shore, or why the jam happened and then cut loose at that time."

He hadn't responded to Katy's question directly because he wasn't sure about his answer. Had he missed his mother? It felt *wrong* that she was gone, and he'd thrown himself into a project that might be able to find her, and fix what had happened, and then—even as it had become increasingly clear that she was gone, her body unrecoverable in the ice floe—had spent more than a decade chasing the spell that hadn't worked because there was such a hole in his life.

But did he *miss* her? Was that what *missing* was? He'd tried to be so busy he *wouldn't* miss her, until he barely *remembered* her.

"I don't know," he said. "I only knew that I had to *fix it*."

Lancelot perked his ears up as the car trembled and jerked beneath them unexpectedly. As Raval sat up straighter, checking the suddenly lit-up instrument panel, the garage exploded around them.

CHAPTER 15

Knowing academically about magic was a lot different from suddenly being transported somewhere unknown in a fiery magical explosion, so Katy thought it was probably understandable that she screamed and clutched at Lancelot.

But as soon as she could, she choked back her ignominious yelp, because they were definitely not in Kansas—or possibly Alaska—any longer.

They were parked in what looked like a convention hall, with short, bold-patterned commercial carpet and big divider panels folded up to one side. Closed double doors before them led…somewhere. There were no windows, but a few overhead exit lights shone enough light that they could see whiteboards and stacks of chairs. There was a podium in one corner. The car had turned off as abruptly as it turned on and the hood was smoking.

"There, there," Raval said awkwardly.

"Are you trying to comfort me?"

"You're scared," he protested. "I can feel it! Sorry, I'm not good at this."

"You're scared too," Katy told him tartly. Then, more kindly, "It's okay. This is kind of a lot. It's totally normal for us to be a little freaked out."

Raval chuckled. "See, you're great at this." He did feel better in her head.

"I have a double certification in reassurance and small talk," Katy joked, peering out the window. Was it safe to get out? Surely, their noisy entrance had not gone unnoticed. Lancelot squirmed in her arms and struggled to stand up in her lap and look out. "Ow, your feet are pointy. Did the magic car work? Are we here to get the kids? Was there just some kind of delay? Is this Amara's evil lair? Because it looks kind of like a hotel."

"I don't know," Raval said, and the last shreds of his concern ebbed away. He was working on a puzzle now, distracted by the questions and *his* ease put Katy at ease.

They got cautiously out of the car and Katy got ahold of Lancelot's leash before he could bolt away.

Raval popped the hood open and waved away the last of the smoke, squinting at the charred writing all over the engine. "The spell is supposed to take the car where it needs to be to fix the activator's problem. I didn't put in constraints, which is why I suspect it didn't work. Maybe the spell figured out just now where it needed to go?"

"Like a slow computer running a complex program? On dial-up?" Katy had no idea what she was looking at.

"The speed of the connection is irrelevant to the speed of the computer," Raval said distantly. "Two very disparate issues. It looks like the car still has some use left in it; nothing appears to have burnt out. And we are probably where we need to be now to rescue the kids. Amara seems to like hotels."

"Well, when you need to house a cult and some kidnapped kids, you probably want room service," Katy said

THE DRAGON PRINCE'S MAGIC

flippantly. It occurred to her that she was not the greatest backup to have on such a mission. "Sorry," she said sheepishly. "Dragons would probably be a lot more useful to have along for this."

Raval frowned at her. "I'm not."

"Not what?" Was he not really a dragon?

"Sorry. That you're here."

Katy could feel a new undercurrent of worry to Raval's curt reply. She wondered if Amara's cult was the kind that had lots of big guns or just a lot of swaying and chanting. It had magic, obviously, but Raval was a magician himself.

"We should figure out where we are," Raval said briskly. He seemed good at stuffing down his worries.

"My phone!" Katy remembered. "Maybe the GPS knows where we ended up." She dug into her purse and thumbed her phone on. "Canada," she announced. She didn't mind Raval leaning close to look over her shoulder and she was glad that he didn't seem to mind the proximity, either. "Northern Ontario. Oh, there's a town named Pickle Lake over there. That's hilarious. Okay, we're about here, in this Fairmont hotel. They have free Wi-Fi, apparently. It looks like we're by an airport. Maybe the sound of airplanes drowned out our arrival."

"I tried to put in some protection contingencies to the spell," Raval suggested. "Maybe we weren't detected."

"Let's go reconnoiter," Katy agreed. "I mean, we'd talked about going on a road trip. It's just as possible that the car just decided we needed a vacation and sent us to the nearest convention hotel with vacancies." She didn't really convince herself.

"Let's assume the worst and try to stay out of sight and under the radar until we're sure either way," Raval cautioned.

But there was immediately a problem with that.

As soon as Lancelot was shut into the car by himself, he

started howling. There was no way it was going to go unnoticed.

"Quiet!" Raval commanded.

"Hush, hush," Katy tried, but Lancelot would have nothing to do with his isolation, scrabbling his paws on the leather molding by the window.

"My car!" Raval said in outrage.

The only way that Lancelot would be quiet was by being on the same side of the car door as they were.

"You should stay here with him," Raval suggested. "It would be safer…"

"We don't know that this isn't just an ordinary hotel," Katy protested, not eager to be left behind. "Lancelot can come exploring with us. Maybe he can defend us," she suggested. "He looks somewhat fierce."

Lancelot sat abruptly down and scratched his ear until he fell over.

"Or not," Katy said.

They did not make the most convincing stealth team.

"Last time we rescued the kids, they were on the top floor," Raval quietly observed. "Let's find a stairwell and go up."

All of Katy's questions about the kind of cult that Amara ran were answered when the stairwell door opened as they approached it and a half-dozen well-armed men and women spilled out, shouting and pointing wicked-looking guns at them.

"It's one of the demon brothers!" one of them shouted.

"No mercy!"

"For the Cause!"

Lancelot gave a happy bark in greeting and strained to the end of his leash. Her shoulder was almost yanked out of its socket because he was much stronger than he looked. Katy turned with a squawk to retreat back to the room they'd come from, for whatever flimsy protection it might offer. Raval, in an act of absolute heroism, stepped in front of her with his arms spread. And Lancelot picked that moment to pull to the side and bring the taut leash to hit the prince in the shins.

Katy thought for a split second that it was going to be a moment from a comedy action movie, where the heroes managed to baffle the goons with their sheer buffoonish antics, but she had forgotten one key thing.

Raval was a dragon.

Like magic, knowing in theory that the members of the royal family were all dragon shifters was a *whole* different thing than watching Raval simply *flow* over Lancelot's leash and explode into a huge sinuous creature that filled the broad hallway and cracked the walls.

He was as gorgeous a dragon as he was a man, with dark shimmering scales over a long, strong body. He had horns and spikes and sharp teeth, with gleaming eyes of silver that seemed as bottomless as galaxies.

He had to keep his wings folded tight in the confined space and he was still the most enormous animal that Katy had ever imagined. He charged down the hallway, smashing rubble from the walls on both sides and raining down acoustic ceiling panels as he bowled over their attackers. Katy heard a rain of gunfire, but Raval's dragon bulk effectively blocked every bullet and he didn't slow down for a moment as he plowed them straight into the firewall at the end of the hall past the stairwell.

Then he was turning, graceful as a dancer and shifting fluidly to human so he could speak. "We're in the right place!" he called. "I'll go find the kids. Get the car ready to go!"

He turned, shifted again, and crashed through the stairwell door. Katy caught a glimpse of a lashing tail and heard more gunshot and shouts as he hurtled up the hotel as a dragon.

"Get the car ready," she echoed, turning away numbly. She tried not to think too hard about the pile of rubble and still figures at the far end of the hall. None of the cultists got up again after they'd been crushed by a dragon against a concrete wall. She squashed her impulse to see if any of them needed help and reminded herself that they were the kind of people who kidnapped little kids and forced them to write magic to destabilize governments.

"Get the car ready," she repeated. There was no way she could catch up with Raval, nor would she be of any help to him whatsoever, particularly saddled with Lancelot, who was still lunging excitedly at the end of his leash. He, at least, seemed completely unfazed by Raval's transformation, or their escalating predicament.

"Get the car ready." Katy ducked back into their conference room parking garage and stared at it. How, exactly, did you get a magic car ready?

She was further thwarted by the fact that Raval had taken the keys with him. Although it wasn't locked, she couldn't get it running even in a *conventional* sense or turn it around, supposing she knew which way she ought to turn it or how they would exit the room. She wasn't sure it would fit through the double doors, and she didn't know how to drive a manual transmission. "Some getaway driver," she muttered to Lancelot, who was happy to jump to put his front paws up on her knees and bounce in place, begging for attention.

Katy's eyes fell on a house phone, clipped to the wall, and she had a burst of inspiration.

If she couldn't get the car ready, maybe she could be of some other use and act as a distraction. She wasn't sure if dragons were entirely bulletproof, but if Amara was a psychopathic cult leader worth her salt, she probably had other protections in place, and Raval might be walking right into a magical trap.

This was an active hotel near an airport, so probably there were other guests here than the cult. Maybe Amara could cast a glamor or something that made her creepy cult look innocuous (nothing to see here but miniature horse enthusiasts!), but that would probably be a lot harder to maintain in the midst of chaos and panic.

So Katy clearly needed to orchestrate some chaos and panic.

She paused at the fire alarm, wondering if she would make things *harder* on Raval, but she could honestly not imagine that anything was going to be more disruptive than a giant lizard rampaging down the halls, and if this could do any small amount to help him, she was going to try. Rather than relying on just the alarm, she also made a panicked call to the front desk on the house phone to report a "raging fire" on the second floor—she almost told them the basement, then decided that she didn't want emergency services finding a car mysteriously parked in one of the convention halls with no apparent entrance that they could have driven in through. She made a second call to 9-1-1 with the same story.

Should she start a real fire? Katy wondered briefly. Then she decided that, as a dragon, Raval was capable of starting his own fire if he wanted one, and she didn't need to risk trapping them all here in an actual blaze.

As she had suspected, the proximity to the airport worked in her favor and it wasn't long before she could hear approaching sirens over the sound of the blaring fire alarm. With luck, they were already evacuating the kids, right into Raval's waiting claws.

CHAPTER 16

Raval surged up the stairwell, swatting aside anyone who got in his way. He took enough bullets to be concerned—dragonhide was tough, but it didn't deflect everything and he was bleeding sluggishly. But he was used to ignoring his body when he had purpose, and he certainly had purpose and focus now.

He had to save the kids, and he had to do it single-handedly, there was simply no one else here to do it and he knew that if he didn't, Katy would be charging in by herself.

A few glaze-eyed tourists staggered into his path as he raged upwards and he slithered past them without pause to the top floor where he hoped to find the kids.

But as it turned out, the kids found him, instead.

The fire alarm started going off when he was at the fifth floor and when he reached the seventh and final floor, the door burst open and he was face-to-face with eleven pajama-clad children holding onto a single ribbon with blocky lettering scribbled all over it.

There was a brief stand-off while Raval tried to decide if

he should shift or if that would leave them too vulnerable to the cultists who must be hot on their heels.

"M-m-mackenzie?" the first child stuttered. "Mackenzie?"

"It's Mackenzie!" another cried in relief.

"We're rescuing ourselves, Mackenzie!"

They thought he was Mackenzie, despite the fact that his dragon form was more green-hued than the princess's, and considerably larger. They probably hadn't seen much of Mackenzie in that form. Rather than dissuade them of their savior, Raval jerked his head back the way that he'd come and squeezed to the side.

"Hold on to the ribbon!" the last girl cried. "If you let go, they'll know we're gone!"

"Go, go!" another cried, and they scrambled down the stairs in a jerky approximation of baby ducklings as Raval covered their tail.

They were not so lucky as to get away unseen. The stairwell door above them ripped open and the children all screamed as bullets rattled down the echoing space. Raval spread his wings, but the bullets only ripped through the membrane and he had a jolt of fear and dismay as the kids fell to the landing and covered their heads.

Someone outside in the hall shouted, "Don't harm the vessels! Don't harm them! She'll have your head!"

"She told me no mercy!" came the reply. "They're useless now!"

Raval turned in the little space, as flexible as a cat, took in a deep breath, and flamed up the stairwell with all his might. There was nothing there to light on fire, but he filled the space with super-heated gas and smoke that would rise and cover their escape.

"Go, go," he yelled, as he shifted back into human form. Several more shots sounded and bullets ricocheted from the walls.

"You're not Mackenzie!" one of the children protested.

"Go!" he snapped, trying to herd them before him. They helped each other to their feet and fled downwards. "Bottom floor," he said, in case he had to shift and pause to protect them before he could tell them where to go. "Conference Hall Twelve! Teacher Katy is there!"

They were painfully slow, with their short human legs and their frightened whimpers, but they obediently went and Raval was starting to think that they might get away with this.

He didn't let himself consider that the car might not take them out again and that they would be trapped in an indefensible hotel basement.

The final flight of stairs was the worst, knowing that they weren't going fast enough, that there was nothing he could do to make them go *faster*.

At some point, the children dropped the ribbon, and it trailed behind them on the steps. Raval stopped to scoop it up, but the words had burned off of it; it was useless now.

The hallway was empty at a glance, but Raval looked the other direction from the conference hall and found that one of the cultists that he'd slammed into the wall was shakily getting up, and he had a strange weapon coming to bear. There were more voices shouting in the stairwell behind him, and sirens, over the blare of the fire alarm.

"I don't know what that weapon will do, and I don't want to!" he hollered at the children and they gave an extra burst of speed to the door where Katy, bless her sweet face, was standing, beckoning them in.

"Get in the car, kids! Fast as you can! There's a puppy in the back, don't untie him! Some of you will have to crawl over the back seat, see who can get there the fastest!"

Raval skidded into the room last and Katy was waiting

with a chair to wedge into the door handles as a make-shift barrier when he slammed it shut behind himself.

"The car isn't running!" he said in alarm. Had it failed to start? Did it need to be running?

"You have the keys!" she retorted. "In, kids! Cindy, Danny, up in the front with me!"

The kids were streaming in like it was a clown car and Lancelot was yipping and licking anything he could reach. Katy shut the door behind the last limb and squeezed in with Cindy and Danny, slamming her door as Raval launched himself over the hood for the driver's seat, fumbling for the keys in his pocket.

He was drawing the driver's door closed as the doors to the hall splintered inward. Shards of wood and broken chair rattled over the windshield.

"Get down! Get down!"

The kids were screaming and flailing limbs, Katy was trying to get them down, and Lancelot was yowling as Raval fumbled the key at the ignition. He didn't feel panicked, but his hands were trembling; he must be more worked up than he realized.

He tried to reassure himself that even if he couldn't get the car to go magically, there was no reason it shouldn't work *physically*, and he might be able to run a few of them down before they could use their weapons. He just had to concentrate and remember how to do it and shut out all the noise and *not freak out.*

Katy's hand on his arm made him realize that he'd stopped trying to get the key in and he looked into her eyes and felt the world stop.

"It's okay," she said, impossibly calm. "I'm here."

And she was. She was there in his head, in his heart. She was the calm and the purpose in the center of the storm, and he had to save her. He had to save her, and the kids, and the howling dog.

Without even looking, Raval put the key in the ignition and turned it, smooth and focused again. "I have to *fix it*," he said.

Around the car, the world exploded.

CHAPTER 17

When Katy could open her eyes, it was utterly dark.

Two of the kids were pressed up against her, clutching whatever they could reach. There was a chin pressed into her side, and sharp little nails in her flesh. The car was filled with panting and whimpering, but none of them were screaming now and Lancelot was only whining.

"Where are we?" one of them finally whispered. Franky, Katy thought, but the voice was so quiet she couldn't exactly tell.

Katy's eyes were getting used to the dimness and she could see that it wasn't *completely* dark.

And they were definitely not in the convention hall any longer. The hood of the car was smoking again, more severely this time, Katy thought. Maybe because there were more people in the car?

"We're in a cave," Paige volunteered, just as it started to resolve for Katy. Were they in caves rumored to be below the Alaskan palace? Those hadn't exactly been part of Katy's orientation tour.

The cavern looked a little too uniform to be completely natural, Katy thought, trying to peel a child off of her so that she could sit up and look out more clearly.

"Raval?"

He was slumped over the wheel of the car. When she reached to touch his arm, he shook her off and sat up. "Where are we?" he asked. "Ow."

"I don't know," Katy said honestly. "The car took us...somewhere."

Raval frowned around and reached for the door latch. "Stay here," he said gruffly.

None of the children volunteered to follow him, but Lancelot barked when he realized that he was being left behind, and squirmed for the front seat so he could follow. He'd slipped his collar, somehow. The children were distracted pulling him back and Raval edged out and shut the door behind him. Katy slid over to the seat that he'd vacated. Cindy and Danny were still clinging to her like leeches, and she could see enough to recognize everyone now. Lancelot had gotten his big paws up on the back of the front seat and he stuck his nose in the back of Katy's neck and snuffled before Randal pulled him gently back.

It was a bit of a wrestling match in the back, Lancelot striving for freedom while the kids were preoccupied trying to keep him under control. Lancelot had moved from whining to husky-specific vocalizations of protest. Katy was glad for the diversion—the kids seemed more interested in the entertainment of a puppy than they were afraid of the threat of Amara or their new, unknown destination.

That meant that Katy was free to worry after Raval, who was lifting the hood of the car. She could feel the prickles of his uncertainty and she reminded herself that he was a dragon, fully capable of facing almost any threat. She could also tell that he was in pain, but she couldn't pick any specifics from it; he seemed to be ignoring it.

"Look, there's a kid!" Lon suddenly exclaimed, and all the kids and Lancelot were immediately riveted to the windows on that side of the car, peering out curiously.

There was a child wearing a simple belted white shirt standing a short distance from the car, close in age to most of Katy's students but very obviously not one of them. He?—she?—was bare-legged and bare-footed.

Raval had been on the far side of the car from the strange child, and he came cautiously around. "Hello?" Katy could barely hear him over the kids in the DeSoto. The child stared back at him and then at the car.

"Who is it?"

"Is it a girl?"

"Who's that?"

"Do you know him?"

"It's a girl!"

"It is not!"

Several of them made exclamations in their first languages.

The kids started out with whispers, but between Lancelot's continued vocalizations and their excitement, they were quickly escalating. Katy glanced at Randal and found that he was focused on the stranger as well. He seemed to be weathering the chaos unexpectedly well, perhaps because there were no expectations whatsoever at this point.

"Wait here," Katy said, unable to stay behind any longer. After all, wasn't childcare her responsibility? She was probably more suited to this kind of diplomacy than Raval was. "No one leave the car."

Lancelot howled again when Katy slipped out and shut the door behind her, but the heavy car body muffled the noise. The air was moist and warm and smelled like salt water. There was a steady strumming that Katy thought was flowing water. They were definitely not in Fairbanks.

"Hello!" she called. "Hello, I'm Katy. Who are you?"

She could feel Raval's relief at her presence. "She won't answer," he said with a shrug.

But the girl—Katy was at least *mostly* sure it was a girl—looked at Katy and smiled slowly. "You aren't where you're supposed to be yet," she chided.

"Where are we?" Raval asked, pouncing. "Where did the car take us?"

"The car takes you back," the girl said sagely, and whatever else she might have said was lost when the door of the car cracked open.

"Teacher Katy? Danny has to pee!"

The crack was enough for Lancelot, in a final, furious bid for freedom, to push open and chaos was utterly unleashed.

The moment he was loose from the car, the husky launched himself straight for the strange girl, who vanished into a sparkle of stars and fleeting feathers.

The rest of Katy's students piled out of the car, all caution lost, and a chase for Lancelot ensued.

"I have to pee!" Danny wailed.

"There's a flashlight in the glove box," Raval said.

Katy took charge of the light source before the children could argue over it, sent Danny to pee behind the car, and called Lancelot. He came, reluctantly, when Katy could get the kids to stop chasing him, and Katy put his collar back on, tighter than before. The children bickered over who could hold Lancelot's leash, and Katy let them figure out their own way to share it.

"There's a word on the wall!" Jessica pointed out, and Katy paused the beam of light on a carved arch. Ornate carved vines twined around a slight recess. Above it was etched the word Truth. It was cleverly shaped into the irregular stone walls, not obvious until she was looking for it.

On a hunch, Katy swung the light around the cavern and found a second, this one twined with flowing water and the word Patience.

It became a game, the kids bouncing ahead of Katy and squinting through the darkness as their eyes adjusted to try to find the next one. The floor was unnaturally flat, Katy thought, and symmetrical, though the ceiling overhead looked organic and there were places she couldn't find the top with the flashlight.

The third alcove was Strength, with mountains carved all around. Then Loyalty, with fire, and Courage, with smoke. The last, behind the car where Danny had already finished, was Kindness, surrounded by clouds and floating flowers.

"I know where we are," Raval said, suddenly at Katy's side. He'd been rummaging under the hood of the car with his cellphone flashlight.

"Not Fairbanks," Katy guessed.

"It's too warm," Cindy said sagely. She was shadowing Katy like a leech.

"Mo'orea," Raval said. His voice sounded raspy, but perhaps it was just the echoes in the cave. "This is where the Renewal of the Compact takes place. These are the virtues of the Small Kingdoms."

"Why did we come here?" Katy asked.

Raval ran his finger through his hair. "The spell on the car isn't specific, you can't assign an actual location. It's supposed to figure out how to fix things."

"Well," Katy said cheerfully, "I guess it did *that*, because it certainly fixed our stuck in the hotel basement problem. My cell phone isn't getting a signal, is yours?"

Raval checked and shook his head. "Nothing," he

confirmed. "Maybe the signal is blocked in the cave." He squinted up. "I thought they had light fixtures in this place."

"There's a beach!"

Danny was standing at a tunnel that ended in light, and all the other children ran to look out with him, exclaiming as they went, as if they were no more than on a grand adventure.

More than a little shaky, Katy went with them, up a slightly sloping path. It was a tall tunnel. Raval could have stood up as a dragon at nearly every point along the way.

The view at the end of it took Katy's breath away, once her eyes adjusted to the brightness, and she heard Raval inhale sharply.

They were in paradise, looking down over a perfect ocean cove. The running water that Katy had heard was a waterfall, cascading just to the side of the cave entrance down into a beautiful lagoon that wandered through a lush jungle to a white sand beach. The air was fragrant with flowers and spices.

"Are we in heaven?" Paige wanted to know.

"Can we go to the beach?" Lon begged.

If they were in Mo'orea, they should be perfectly protected and safe, Katy thought. Mo'orea and Alaska were allies, and she'd heard nothing but good stories about Leinani's home. "Stay out of the water!" she warned.

Lancelot chose that moment to give a mighty lunge at the end of his leash and pull it from Danny's grip, which precipitated a mad dash of the children down the path towards the beach.

"I'm so slow," Raval said. He was turned away from Katy, one hand out in the spray from the waterfall. "The car couldn't work any earlier, because the kids hadn't broken themselves out yet. We wouldn't have had a chance getting past Amara's protections, but they could do it themselves and when they did, we were able to go get them."

Katy realized that through her own considerable shock, she was feeling Raval's confusion and his sudden awareness of pain. "Raval?"

As she reached for him, Raval nearly pitched forward off the little landing they were standing on trying to avoid her, and when he turned to her, she saw what she had not been able to make out in the darkness of the cave: his shirt was blooming with blood.

"You were shot!"

Raval looked down at himself in wonder. "I guess I was," he agreed in surprise. "It's not too bad," he assured her. "You shouldn't worry so much."

Glad that the kids had already moved along, Katy drew Raval aside and had him sit beside the path on a convenient mossy log. "Take off your shirt."

It wasn't as bad as Katy had feared from the quantity of blood that his white shirt had soaked up, but he had a dozen little wounds across his chest and shoulders.

"Are the bullets still in there?" Katy asked in concern. "Do I have to suck them out? No, that's rattlesnake poison, but seriously, you should see a doctor." She dug her phone out of her purse and found that she still didn't have any signal. "Do you know where on Mo'orea we are? What's the nearest town? Can we walk there?"

"That's the weird part," Raval said, as she hesitantly poked at one of the sluggishly bleeding holes. "We ought to be able to see the capital city, just across the bay there."

Katy lifted her head and peered at the distant spit of land that stretched out into the turquoise sea. "I don't see any buildings."

"I've been here," Raval said. "You should be able to see the city skyline from here, clear as day."

"There's no city there," Katy said in confusion. Had being shot given Raval a *concussion?*

"There's no city there *yet*," Raval corrected.

Katy stared at him. "Yet?!"

"This is Mo'orea," Raval said confidently. "This is the mouth of Opunohu Bay. But the city hasn't been built yet."

CHAPTER 18

Raval didn't think that he liked being fussed over, but he found that he liked it when Katy fussed over him. Her hands never felt like too much touch, and he enjoyed having her close. They could hear the kids and Lancelot, shouting to each other and barking as they explored the beach below them.

"I don't think there are any bullets left inside," he told Katy, because even the shocking revelation of their destination hadn't eased her worry for him. "I should heal up quickly and be fine."

"Then what's worrying you?" Katy pressed. "I mean besides the fact that we've apparently traveled back in time."

"The car," Raval admitted, now that the kids were all out of earshot. "It's broken. I don't think it can take us back."

"Is that why it brought us here, er, now? There was something wrong with the spell?"

"I don't think that it was a problem with the spell that did this," Raval clarified. "But the magic that was required to bring us here burned out big parts of the text. I'm going to have to re-write them, from scratch in a few places."

Katy blinked at him. "That sounds complicated," she said with admirable serenity. Raval could feel the self-control that it took—she felt shocky and unsettled and Raval wasn't used to being the comforting one.

"It will be," he said, as calmly as he could manage. "And it will take a long time."

Katy gave a little hiccup of a laugh that was a shadow of her usual chuckle. "Well, apparently time travel is a thing, so we might not even be missed. How...how long? For us, I mean, considering we might end up only a few minutes later than we left?"

Raval thought about the damage he'd seen under the hood, all the smeared lettering and burnt out commands. He wouldn't want to rush it and make things worse. "A few months," he guessed. "Give or take."

Katy let out a shaky breath. "Okay," she said, though Raval could tell it wasn't. "Okay," she repeated more firmly. "We'll need food, we'll need shelter. This waterfall should provide clean water, it looks like it comes straight from the mountain top, and the cave can protect us from rain. As places to be stuck in the past go, this probably isn't awful. There should be fruit here, and fish, and February in prehistory Alaska would be a lot colder and less fun. Let's assess what tools we've got. I've got a multi-tool in my purse, and a few snack bars. Do you have a toolbox in the car?"

"I've got a toolbox and a survival kit," Raval volunteered. "With a few MREs and a solar-powered radio and charger."

"What made you put a survival kit in a vintage car?" Katy asked.

"I live in Alaska," Raval said sensibly. "You should always be prepared. I mean, I'm a dragon, but you never know who you'll need to help out."

Her laugh was more genuine and Raval could feel that the shock was starting to pass.

"You are the very best kind of prince," she said. "I don't think you're even bleeding any more. Let's mop you up and get this shirt rinsed out before the blood sets. I don't think they have stain remover in whatever century we're in."

"I'm going to go scout around the island," Raval declared, testing his range of movement. "You should make sure the kids aren't going too *Lord of the Flies* down there."

Katy laughed and Raval was startled to realize that it was a decent joke, if grim. "Try not to get shot at again," she cautioned him with a kiss. "If they even have guns in this time."

Raval tried to remember when the Mo'orea capital city had been moved; he'd never been that keen on history. "I have no idea if they do," he admitted. "I'll be careful."

That made her feel better and Raval stepped away so he had enough room to shift and kick off from the little landing by the tunnel without hitting her.

It was easiest to fly in cold air, but Raval was still able to lift off with ease; the tears in his membrane were minor and not more than annoying. He wouldn't want to have to fly a long distance, but he was fine for a brief tour of the island; it wasn't that large.

There were settlements, on the opposite side of the heart-shaped island, several bustling little villages. Raval didn't want to get too close, concerned about unknowingly disrupting the timeline, so he stayed high and away. He tried to gauge their technology from that height and get an idea of *when* they were. He guessed that they were pre-industrial, but that didn't narrow it down much. There were some large buildings and there was smoke from a few chimneys. That probably wasn't for warmth, but might be necessary for crafting or cooking.

A pod of dolphins noticed him, leaping and calling, but he

went unobserved by the other locals. If there were dragons, he didn't see them.

He swooped down along the coast, observing the terrain with an eye for things they could eat and build with, as well as possible dangers. The volcano appeared to be long-dormant and there was not a single sign of predators. Flocks of lazy seabirds were nesting unconcerned on rocky shores, and long, untouched white sand beaches were dappled in shadows of swaying palm and fruit trees.

There were great reefs protecting the island in all directions—the waves that reached the shores were lazy and low, and Raval could see thick schools of fish sheltering in the shallows. Fishing and gathering eggs should be simple.

Something caught his eye and Raval angled out over the ocean to a far corner of the reef. There was a shipwreck, half-submerged in the rocks there. It was an ancient Chinese junk, Raval thought, from what remained of the hull. Large parts of its sails still remained and Raval realized it might make good salvage for tents or sun shelters. He feared it would be too thick for clothing, but maybe the children's pajamas would last until he could fix the car.

He made a mental note to return to the wreck for whatever he could save, but his chest was aching now and his flight was less efficient than it would be with whole wings. He knew that Katy would be angry with him if he overextended himself, so he angled back to the beach he'd come from.

CHAPTER 19

Katy wondered if she would always feel a little bereft when Raval left, or if that was just a function of the mate bond.

It was bizarre watching him change into a dragon and then leap into the air. He seemed to shimmer and disappear into the brightness of the sky. Knowing where he'd gone, Katy could see a little smudge to the sky where he was at first, but it was fleeting and confusing. She lost sight of him quickly.

She wadded his bloody shirt into her hands, not wanting to draw attention to it and horrify the kids, and went to find out if they had descended to cannibalism.

The path from the tunnel to the beach was overgrown, like it hadn't been used in many years, though Katy suspected that things grew faster here in the all-summer season than plants in Alaska. The waterfall fell into a narrow finger of water that looked like a tidal pool, and Katy walked along it, pushing foliage out of the way, until she got to the thinner forest that edged the big crescent beach.

Lancelot came racing to meet her, flailing whenever he hit soft sand, and the children swiftly followed.

"Lon caught a fish!" Danny announced.

"It got away," the boy sheepishly admitted.

Jessica told her, "Jamie found bananas!"

"I fell in the water!"

"I don't think that being wet will hurt you," Katy said to Jin comfortingly.

"It's warm," he agreed.

"Can we stay a little bit?" Cindy asked.

"I want to go swimming," Paige said longingly.

They milled around her, eager for direction, and Katy remembered Raval's dismay. A month. Maybe two. "We might be here for a while," she said, hoping it sounded like a treat and not a threat. "Let's set up a camp!"

The kids cheered and scattered to follow her commands.

"Go get everything from the car," she told Randal and Taxina. "Let's take stock of what we have. We'll need a fire pit, and firewood. Prit? Jin? And we'll want something to sit on. Paige, can you gather some of that driftwood with Franky? We can sleep in the cave tonight if it rains, but it might be nicer on the beach. Let's gather some leaves to make into beds! Jessica, can you and Jamie go get some of the bananas you found?"

They each scrambled away as soon as they got orders. Katy let Cindy direct the layout of their little camp, choosing a spot in a clearing of the trees for their fire and pointing out places for each of them to sleep.

Katy reminded her to pick a place away from the camp for an outhouse. "We'll have to dig a hole for it later! Gather some soft leaves for toilet paper, too!"

This elicited a lot of groans and *ews*!

The sun was still high, but Katy remembered that nightfall came fast in the tropics, and she wanted to be ready. She went to the edge of the tidal pool and washed what she could of the blood from Raval's shirt and jacket. The jacket didn't show a stain, but his shirt, besides being riddled with holes, would never be white again. She hung them on a bush in the sun to dry out.

Randal and Taxina came down from the cave with their arms heaping and Katy spread everything out on her parka to take stock.

Raval's survival kit was minimal but looked very useful, with a knife that she gave to Cindy for stripping down leaves, three MREs, a first aid kit, and a whistle she had to immediately confiscate. There was a solar-powered radio-flashlight-phone charger that got no signal, anywhere on the dial. Randal sat down with this and patiently tested every channel, over and over again.

Katy upended her purse, and found several packs of gum, a multi-tool, a pill case, a sewing kit, hair ties, a pair of sunglasses, a tiny packet of tissue, six snack bars, and a worn paperback with a shirtless man on the cover, plus an assortment of receipts, breath mints, paperclips, and a wide-toothed comb.

"Can we make a fish hook out of the paperclips?" Lon wanted to know, peering over her shoulder.

"I think it might be easier to make a dip net," Katy said thoughtfully. "The fish are as dense here as a salmon run and we can wade right out into them!"

Lon nodded solemnly. "Maybe a spear," he said with relish.

By the time Raval returned, appearing out of a shimmer in the coloring sky and landing hard on the sand, they had eked out the bustling skeleton of a camp.

"You got a lot done while I was gone," he observed when he'd shifted back to human and been given an exuberant tour.

There was a little pile of coconuts and small bananas, plus a heaping stack of dry firewood by a rock-ringed fire pit with a pile of tinder and kindling. They had gathered up driftwood seats all around it.

"I don't have a lighter," Katy said, standing up to give Raval a kiss. "Then I remembered that you were a dragon. But the kids are trying to do it themselves."

Paige was gamely trying to make flame by rubbing two sticks together. Several others were bending over her, trying to be encouraging.

"I think I see smoke!"

"No, you don't!"

"It's smoking!"

"No, it's not!"

Raval cleared his throat. "I can light that," he suggested. "Give me some space." The children retreated from the fire pit with wide eyes and whispers.

It would never get old watching him flow into dragon form, Katy thought with a shiver of awe. A tiny, focused bolt of flame lit the waiting wood and—except for Paige, who pouted—they cheered and gathered to feed it more sticks and logs.

"Triumph!" Katy said.

Raval shifted back again.

"What did you find?" she asked, as he came to sit beside her on one of the gathered driftwood seats. "Lon, don't put that in yet, you'll smother the fire!"

"There's a big shipwreck out past the breakers," Raval said. "I can probably salvage some canvas sail for some shelter, maybe some rope or big beams. I didn't want to do too much until I'd healed some more because I knew you'd scold me."

"I would," Katy agreed. "And...people?"

THE DRAGON PRINCE'S MAGIC

"There are a few villages on the other side of the island, not very advanced, from what I could tell."

"You didn't make contact?"

Raval shook his head. "I'm not sure how much we want to mess with the past. If we really need something, we can try talking to them, but it might be best to disturb as little as possible of the timeline."

"We don't want to be making a bunch of paradoxes," Katy agreed. "Did you know that your car could do this?"

Raval was quiet and Katy could feel the conflict in his head. She restrained her instinct to touch him and let him chew through it in his own time. "I knew it might," he said at last. "I was thinking a lot about *going back* and *fixing it*. But I tried to add a lot of spell parts to keep it from *messing things up*. I wasn't sure if that would be enough to make it work. And I'm not sure why it took us here. This wasn't any time that I was thinking of."

"Well, we probably won't starve, while you get it running again," Katy assured him. "We've got lots of fruit, there are plentiful fish to catch.

"Teacher Katy?" Cindy said plaintively into their conversation. "We're hungry."

Katy stood briskly. "It's starting to get dark, and it's too late for fishing tonight." Lon gave a groan of disappointment. "Let's divide the snack bars and Jamie's bananas and we'll tackle gathering food in earnest tomorrow morning when it's light again."

The moon, which had been a faint semicircle in the sky that afternoon, brightened as the sun went down, and cast enough light for them to finish their scant meal and find their beds.

"I want to stay up," Franky complained.

Cindy answered before Katy could. "We have to go to bed

to get up early because we're kids and we need sleep and have to get up early. Don't complain."

Katy shooed them all to their rustling piles of leaves and paused to give each one of them a kiss on their head. Lancelot did the rounds with her and finally thumped down to lie with Randal, to his deep delight.

She returned to the fire to find Raval covering the coals in sand. "The kids made us a bed, too," she told him quietly. "It's probably pretty lumpy and itchy and small and has no privacy."

"Just one bed, huh?" he said wryly.

He took her hand when she offered it and she led him to the "master bedroom" that Cindy had directed. He willingly lay down with her, wrapping his arms around her. He was warm and solid, in a world that had come undone at the seams, and Katy let herself relax into him and embrace her exhaustion. It wasn't so cool, even with the sun down, that she feared that they would suffer from exposure, but she also wasn't surprised to hear the kids whispering and fidgeting and moving their beds around. She fully expected to find them all sleeping in one pile by morning.

She lay awake a long while, too tired to sleep, and wondered if time travel counted as *other duties as required.* She should have negotiated for a higher salary.

CHAPTER 20

Raval would have made faster progress on the car if he had not been indispensable for so much of the work around their camp. He could reach fruit from high in the trees and easily break down branches or whole trees for their building projects. He could quickly dig into the sand with his claws to do what would be hours of work for the kids with their makeshift shovels. He could frighten entire schools of fish into the waiting nets of the kids as they stood knee-deep in the water shrieking in triumph.

Raval salvaged several huge portions of oiled canvas sail from the sunken ship, and long beams that became the base of four sturdy tents—one for the girls, one for the boys, one as a food and storage tent, and one small one set a little ways away for Raval and Katy. He found a small portion of netting tangled in some floating jetsam.

It didn't rain often, but when it did, they were cozy and comfortable in their shelters, and the island provided ample food. Raval grudgingly handed over all four hubcaps from the Firestorm to be hammered into shallow bowls that could be filled with water and heated over the fire. They gathered wild bird eggs and cooked fish on spikes or wrapped in palm leaves and buried with hot rocks.

If they weren't always full, they were never very hungry for long, and they had everything that they strictly needed, with the bonus of a number of unexpected luxuries. Lon won a honeycomb with a dozen bee stings, and Jessica found a deposit of salt that was the finest spice they'd ever had on the many varieties of fish that filled their days. Tidepools provided a variety of crabs and mussels. Katy figured out how to make a crude soap out of ashes and fish oil, cheering out loud when it lathered up.

They even diverted some of the fresh water from the waterfall to their little camp, using a series of half-logs that Raval hollowed out with his claws. It was a leaky, wasteful construct, but it allowed them to establish a crude washing and drinking system.

It didn't take long to figure out the best greenery to dry for soft bedding and Raval's uniform coat and Katy's parka were disassembled, every little piece put to use. The kids' pajamas held up better than they'd feared, carefully patched with the precious thread in the tiny sewing kit. Sleeves were ripped off and repurposed as patches and satchels, and every inch of the heavy canvas sail was useful.

Only Raval had boots. Katy's shoes were useless in sand and the kids didn't even have slippers, but running everywhere barefoot seemed no hardship and their soles got tough.

They didn't have any blankets, but the cool night air didn't bother Raval, and he kept Katy warm. The children slept together for warmth, Lancelot a coveted companion among the kids for both his affection and his steam engine heat during the night.

Katy and the children worked on his training, and Lancelot willingly learned tricks for coveted pieces of fish, but remained stubborn about recall techniques. Fortunately, he didn't seem inclined to wander too far, and there were no predators on the island for him to tangle with.

The husky shed his winter coat and started to grow into his big feet as the kids turned brown in the sun and their hair got shaggier and shaggier. Raval's facial hair went through an itchy stage and then settled into a scruffy beard that Katy declared that she loved. She was unabashed about her own body hair.

Every morning, Raval set the flashlight to recharge on the sluggish little solar charger and did a lot of the work that only a dragon could do…or at least, that a dragon could do the easiest. Then he'd take the flashlight to work on the car, laboriously trying to reconstruct the thirteen years of work that had burned away.

Not all of it was gone, of course, but enough that he knew the spell wouldn't work. He had to try to remember what he'd written before, connecting all the parts that remained. In some ways, it was more challenging than writing it all from scratch.

Some days, the bright little fae spirit child was there in the cave, watching him and sometimes making obscure comments that didn't seem to stay in his memory very long, like her words were slippery.

Sometimes, one of the children came to help him.

"It must be cool to be a dragon," Danny told him. The smallest of the boys, for some reason he had attached himself to Raval. He was constantly bringing him drinks in hollowed out coconut shells and showing him shells that he'd found on the beach and telling long, rambling stories about things that Raval could find no sense in.

Although Raval didn't particularly encourage the boy, he did find that he could be helpful in holding the flashlight for the car while he worked, even if he had to remind the child several times every hour that he couldn't work as well while Danny was talking.

"I want to be able to fly," Danny said enviously. "Swoosh! Swoosh! What's it like?"

Raval was never sure which questions were serious and which were rhetorical, so he answered them all. "It's all I know," he explained. "I've always had a dragon in my head with me, so I don't know what it's like to not have one. I do like flying."

"Is it like always having a friend?" Danny asked wistfully. "Lon was supposed to be my friend, but he's friends with Jin now and Cindy says that it's okay if we're not always the same kind of friends with each other but I kind of miss him."

Raval didn't have a lot of experience with children and their relationships, but he suspected that these eleven kids had less drama than most young people of their age would have, and it was still plenty. He dredged the question out of the rambling. "It *is* like always having a friend," he said. "Sometimes, he tells me what people are expecting me to say or do. And he understands magic better than I do."

"He sounds *smart*," Danny said. Then, smugly, "Jin isn't as smart as me."

"I need to concentrate now," Raval reminded him. That would buy him another ten minutes of quiet.

It wasn't entirely easy living. Cindy stepped on a wicked thorn that pierced her foot. Katy applied a tiny packet of expired antibiotic cream from the first aid kit to it, but it still turned red and swelled up. Cindy spent a day complaining and limping, then a worrisome, tense day being entirely too quiet, off-color and feverish, until Raval was contemplating taking her to the village on the other side of the island to see what they could do for her, timeline be damned.

But the following morning, she bounced back full of energy, and she spent the next several days ruling the children from a driftwood throne as they waited on her while she kept her foot dramatically elevated.

Raval built them a playground, because they were kids and he remembered that they ought to be able to play. A teeter-totter was simple, and a swing. He considered sacrificing the spare tire for the Firestorm as a tire swing, but he thought they might need it, and while he suspected that he could get it off the rim fairly easily, putting it back on without tools would be challenging.

Fortunately, they'd never been on a playground, so they had no expectations for it. The slide was not as slippery as Raval had hoped, but the kids could ride down it on big palm leaves. He couldn't figure out how to make a merry-go-round with the supplies they had, but it was simple to make an obstacle course with things to climb on and chase around.

He even played with them, reluctantly at first, then more easily. They swam together in the lagoon and he would toss them into the deepest water with his snout. He didn't mind them dog-piling onto him, playing a watery king-of-the-dragon, and he didn't hesitate to shake them all loose, laughing and splashing.

Their touch didn't bother him through dragonskin.

It was a long, endless summer and Raval felt himself fall into a pleasant rhythm of routine, interspersing work and play in perfect measure. With Katy at his side, her heated touches and her heart-warming smiles, he felt like he was a king of their little island paradise and he wasn't actually sure that he ever wanted it to end.

CHAPTER 21

Katy stared at the ocean.

She didn't have many moments free to herself to pause and think. She was constantly gathering food or working on the improvements for their tiny makeshift village. She tried to keep up with lessons, scratching math problems into leaves and using pebbles and sticks in the sand to explain fractions and geometry. They used the scientific method to analyze their little world. The physics they studied was by practical application, exploring levers and water flow with their crude plumbing. The only book she had was a wholly inappropriate romance novel that had been in her purse, so she relied on oral story-telling from her memory of the age-appropriate classics.

The kids were increasingly independent, and they ranged much further here than they would have been allowed in their own time and place, but they still wanted a lot of attention from her, eager to show off the skills they were learning and all their little triumphs and discoveries. They grew brown-skinned and rangy, developing muscles that they'd never cultivated in their previous life.

Katy tried to spend the free time that she did get alone with Raval.

Sometimes, they snuck off and made love in the back of the car, or in their tiny tent. Sometimes, they talked about magic, Raval bouncing ideas off of her and refining his work. Sometimes, she just held the flashlight and quietly watched him etch letter after careful letter into the car. She made sure that he ate and rested at appropriate intervals, and dragged him out to walk along the beach with her in the morning before the sun got too high.

She could feel the mate bond slowly fading, in the same weird way that the kids were getting taller whenever she looked away and Lancelot was growing into his ears. It didn't happen all at once, but Katy knew that it was slipping and wanted to cling to it as long as she could.

Their life on the island was busy, but joyful. There were no predators to fear, and fruit and fish were plentiful. Their hard work led to hard play, with regular bonfires on the beach. They celebrated every little win with all their hearts.

But something was different now. There was a new urgency nagging at Katy, a little flutter of worry that she couldn't quite contain.

She thought that it was a sure sign that the mate bond was almost gone that Raval didn't pick up on her concern, and after chewing over it like a dog on a bone for several days, she knew that she needed to tell him her concerns outright.

"Paige said you wanted to talk to me. What do you need?"

From anyone else, it would seem like an insensitive greeting. He didn't start with words of endearment or courtesy. But that was just Raval, and Katy knew that he would appreciate her getting to the point as well. If she could figure out *how*.

"Sit with me, this might take a moment."

THE DRAGON PRINCE'S MAGIC

The kids had put together a broad bench of driftwood, just high of the high tide mark on the beach, and they sat there now, a careful space between them. Raval loved to be touched, but found it distracting during conversations.

He didn't rush her, as Katy tried to put together her jumbled thoughts. "I know that you've been working hard on the car," she started.

No, that wasn't where she wanted to start.

"Bodies...do things," she tried.

That was no better.

"We don't have everything we might need here, in this time."

Raval was looking at her blankly. "Things we need for...bodies?"

Katy was pretty sure that she was breaking this news in the worst possible way. "Right."

Raval nodded. "The girls. They're growing up. They'll hit puberty and have periods. That's going to be messy—I've seen the commercials. What do we need for that? Is there something we can make pads from? I mean, it would be more ideal to just get back to our own time sooner than later, I suppose."

Katy wasn't sure if she loved Raval's frankness more, or the fact that he could face the prospect of being stuck on an island with a half dozen girls getting periods for the first time with utter, unflappable aplomb.

"It isn't about periods," she said, not quite able to keep from laughing. Then she sobered. "Well, it sort of is. But it's about *mine*."

Raval followed that train of thought logically. "You'll need something, too, I hadn't thought..."

Katy saw the moment that he realized how much time had passed since they got there and figured out the connection she'd already made. He didn't flinch or smile or laugh or look shocked or glad or unhappy, but his eyes blinked faster, and there was a little jerk to the muscle at his neck.

"Oh." He took a few breaths and swallowed.

"I don't know for sure," Katy hastened to tell him. "We weren't keeping track at first, so I don't know exactly how long we've been here. I ran out of pills a few weeks ago, but they aren't infallible, so it might have even been before that. And it could just be nutritional, or maybe time travel plays havoc with menstrual cycles, and I've never been perfectly regular to start with, so…"

"A baby," Raval breathed.

Katy took in a shaky breath of her own. "A baby. Maybe." She braced herself for his reaction.

CHAPTER 22

A baby.
Raval's brain was doing that thing where it was stuck in a loop, and he recognized it, and there was still nothing he could do about it.

A baby, his dragon thought once, delighted. But Raval couldn't *stop* thinking about it.

A baby. Katy's baby. *His* baby. A baby *they* made.

Who would trust him with a baby? What do you do with a baby? Raval wasn't sure he'd ever even held a baby. Fask was the one who always did the kissing infants sort of thing for the press and Raval wasn't usually even invited to show up at press conferences—he was a middle brother of no consequence.

And now, there might be a baby.

A *baby*.

Katy's baby.

His baby.

A baby *they* made.

He was a record on a skip, back to the start, with all the shock and alarm and terror of the very first pass.

And it wasn't all bad, he realized, after a few iterations. He guessed it would be loud and messy and a lot of trouble, but there was something appealing about a baby with Katy, about the idea of Katy holding their baby, about snuggling down with a baby between them. They would watch it grow up together. Would it be mechanically apt, like he was? Or big-hearted and humorous, like Katy?

A baby.

Katy's baby.

His baby.

A baby they made.

Raval only realized that he should be saying something comforting to Katy when he felt her concern and recognized that he had been staring at her without speaking for some time. What was one supposed to say at a time like this? Something sage that implied he'd be a good father? Something to assure Katy that he'd be the best partner he could imagine?

His dragon was not helpful, just happily content with the idea of a baby, and a nest, and starting a hoard for it.

"A baby," Raval said.

Saying it out loud released some of the pressure building inside of him and Katy smiled at him in relief.

"I know it's not the best timing," she said. "I'd rather do this in a time with hospitals and antibiotics and stuff. Basic hygiene. Disposable diapers. Pickles and ice cream."

"I have to fix the car," Raval said firmly, as if that hadn't been the first thing on his mind every day anyway. It was even more urgent now. "Because there's a baby."

"Maybe," Katy cautioned. "I mean…probably. But I can't know for sure and I needed you to know there was a chance. A pretty good chance."

"I like that you tell me things," Raval said honestly. "Even

THE DRAGON PRINCE'S MAGIC

when you don't want to, you tell me and then I know instead of guessing wrong."

Katy's face was so dear to him, in all of its baffling expressions, but it was dearest of all when she smiled at him like this, unmistakably happy, and he knew he'd just said everything right for once.

"I'm not sorry," Raval told her, in case she was still worried that he might be disappointed. He could tell that she was worried, but he couldn't decide if it was just because they were stuck back in time before doctors on an island in the middle of nowhere, or if she had worries about his reaction. Worries just looked like worries, without instructions or direction, and he ought to forestall any that he could. "I like the idea, though it does come with a great deal of..." he flapped his hand, not sure if it would be diplomatic to say a baby was a hassle.

Because whatever else he knew about babies, he knew they were a hassle.

And he knew that he had to do what he could to make it better for Katy, and that meant taking them all back to the future where they belonged, where it was *safer* for a pregnant woman and a new baby.

He was so focused on his task that he forgot that Katy would want a kiss before he went back to work, and he was glad when she caught him as he turned back for the cave and drew him down to press her lips to his.

A baby.

Katy's baby.

His baby!

A baby they made!

If they hadn't already started one, Raval rather thought they might right then, based on the heat of her kiss and the eagerness of her body against his, but one of the kids—Cindy—came skidding up to say, "Ew! Teacher Katy, Franky found a jellyfish on the beach and he says it won't sting but I said it would and Paige says that you pee on jellyfish stings but that's just an old wives tale and Lon won't stop poking it and Jamie is *crying*."

Lancelot danced around at her feet, growling and falling onto his elbows because running places meant *playing*, and although he was starting to grow into his huge feet, he was still very much a puppy.

Katy peeled herself out of Raval's arms, to his disappointment, and gave a tolerant laugh. "I'll come have a look and we'll see what I remember about jellyfish and we'll help Jamie feel better."

"I'll fix the car," Raval said, letting her go. They needed to get back to their own time more than ever now.

Because there was a baby.

Katy's baby.

His baby!

A baby they made!

It was always rough going back to a magic project after a break, which was why Raval was often cross about having to stop for food and biological needs, and why he especially resented being interrupted.

He lifted the hood to the DeSoto and stared down at the engine. His awl was getting dull, and there was no chance of finding more steel hard enough to chisel into the engine block in this time period, and he didn't have a grinder to erase mistakes, so he was trying to conserve what he wrote, thinking every word and letter through before he started it.

Magic was always demanding and took very careful, intent thought, with no distractions or side trips.

And now there was something else occupying his mind.

A baby.

There was no escaping it, so Raval rode the obsession instead, using it to focus his magical skill, to incorporate this new urgency as a part of the spell. He had to get them back to where it was safe. He had to think of every loophole for chaos and close it. He had to protect the kids, and Katy, and that ridiculous dog...and their baby.

A baby.

Katy's baby.

His baby.

A baby they made.

CHAPTER 23

It took two more weeks for Raval to finish the spell, scratching it laboriously into the parts of the car that he hadn't already set magic into. Katy brought him meals in the cave and made him a bed by the car where he could snatch a few hours of sleep when his body's exhaustion was too much. He only saw the sun a few times when she dragged him out to swim and bathe.

"You can't keep doing this," Katy protested, when he woke up to find her hovering over the makeshift bed. Raval couldn't remember when he'd last let her feed him. The end of a spell was always the most intense, and he'd pushed her firmly away the last few times she tried to interrupt.

"It's done," he said, feeling like he'd lost a part of himself.

He waited for the feeling of Katy's delight and relief and when he did, it was so faint and far off that he realized that the mate bond must finally have faded away while he was intent on the spell.

It was only his *own* delight and relief in his head, for being finished, and it was drowned in the fear and despair that followed.

He'd never know what she felt again. He wouldn't have that vital clue that let him understand her. That delicious trust and compassion that he'd felt with her was gone forever and she could never want him now, now that magic wasn't rubbing off all the rough edges of him. He didn't know how to *tell* her things that she'd been able to feel from him.

Was this the end of them?

When she realized that connection was lost, why would she want to stay with him?

Where did a baby fit now?

She was clapping her hands in delight now, which probably meant that she hadn't noticed that he couldn't feel her emotions any longer. He would have to muddle through and pretend, for as long as he could, because it would break her precious heart to know that he was back to flat, heartless Raval, and he couldn't bear to hurt her.

"It's done," he repeated, because it would make her happy. He had to hope it would, anyway. "We can go whenever you want."

"You are a genius," she told him, kissing him as he sat up. "A sexy genius." It was still easy to hold her in his arms. They had practiced so much that it was automatic, almost instinctive. He cradled her close and tried to soak in the feeling while he could. She was so perfect there. So perfect, and so fleeting.

Then she wrinkled her nose and drew back. "A *smelly* genius," she scolded him. "Have a quick snack and go swim the sweat off of you in the cove. We'll have a feast, and use everything up because we'll be back in Alaska tonight, with fast food if we want it. Oh heavens, I can't wait for a French fry again. Or a bagel. I would do violence for a corn chip. Next time you hurdle us back into the past, hit a time when they had taco stands, would you?"

Raval laughed, because she had always loved it when he did that, and besides, she was always very funny.

Then he obediently ate the banana she gave him, shucked off his clothing so that she could wash it, and went to swim out into the crystal clear cove and let the salt water waves scrub the last of the magic from the corners of his mind.

When he was done floating and had rinsed the salt from his body at the waterfall, Raval dressed again in sun-dried clean clothing that was only barely damp and found that the kids had taken the idea of a feast to a new level.

The driftwood table they had built was draped in the fabric that Jamie had painstakingly woven from palm fronds and grasses, and it was decorated all over with shells and flowers. Every lamp that they'd made was spread out on it, though it wasn't really dark enough to light them yet, and the dishes were heaped with fish and boiled roots and all the ways of cooking bananas that they had invented. The carved cups were filled to the brim with pulpy juice, and all the kids pointed out the parts of the feast that they'd contributed, even Randal, who had done the juicing.

They hadn't talked about going home in weeks, but they did that night.

"What do you guys miss most?" Katy asked. "I have to admit I miss television. I have no idea who Alaska's Next Top Singer is, or who won the Canadian Maple Bake-Off."

The kids shrugged, and it occurred to Raval that they hadn't really enjoyed a lot of modern conveniences or media. They'd only been at the palace a few weeks before their unceremonious recapture, and before that, they'd been imprisoned without entertainment by Amara. Being stranded on a deserted island was probably not as much of a lifestyle change as going from the cult to a castle had been.

"I miss the books," Randal offered thoughtfully.

"I miss my rabbit," Cindy said, as if it shamed her.

"I miss ice cream," Jamie said.

Jessica just agreed with everyone else, nodding her head vigorously.

"Indoor toilets," Raval said, when they looked at him. "And toilet paper."

That, of course, led to a lot of embarrassed giggling and bodily function jokes that increased in intensity until Katy chided them, laughing, and told them to keep the discussion appropriate for a meal.

"I miss Mackenzie," Paige said sadly, when the laughter had died down.

The sun was just starting its madcap descent into the ocean. Raval wondered how time travel would work. Would they go back to where they'd left? Had anyone missed them? Was it night there, or day? If it was February in Alaska still, it would have gotten dark mid-afternoon. But maybe it was March, or even April. "Want to go see Mackenzie now?" he offered.

They mopped up the camp swiftly, leaving it tidy, with everything cleaned and put away, as if they were going to wake up the next morning and use it all again, even though Raval really hoped that they wouldn't.

Most of the kids chose to take a few of their handmade treasures, and Jamie folded her woven tablecloth and tucked it into the back of the DeSoto. The kids wandered around, saying goodbye to the playground equipment that they'd built and their favorite fruit trees. Lancelot danced around, completely underfoot, like he knew that they were leaving, and he was determined not to be left behind. The husky grew distressed every time that he lost sight of any of the kids, yowling and trying to herd them like sheep.

"Everyone go to the bathroom before we leave," Katy warned them, as if they were merely going on a long, normal roadtrip. They even packed snacks, on the chance that they didn't end up where they wanted to be.

The little spirit child was waiting in the cavern for them, perched at the top of the Patience alcove, and she waved forlornly, but didn't offer to come down and see them off.

"Load up," Katy finally said, and they all wedged into the sprawling old car and held on to whatever they could as Raval sucked in a breath and slipped into the driver's seat opposite from her. Cindy and Danny, as the smallest, were wedged between them.

"Is it going to work?" Cindy asked, with deep skepticism.

"I hope so," Raval said honestly.

Have faith, his dragon reminded him.

Raval put the key in the ignition, placed both his hands on the steering wheel, and spoke the words that had brought them here: *"I have to fix it."*

The car roared to life, echoing in the cave, and the headlights came on with such bright intensity that Raval had to shield his eyes and he saw Katy do the same as everything jerked and pulled and seemed to explode.

Just as Raval could open his eyes again, the car sputtered and died and the lights blinked out, leaving nothing but an after-impression of the cave walls around them.

They were still in the cave and Raval felt his heart drop.

"It didn't work," Lon whined. "We're still here."

"Maybe we're in the right time?" Katy said, with her cheerful, uncrushable optimism. "Does your phone get a signal?"

As Raval reached to turn on his phone, he caught sight of two lights, high in the cave and had a moment of hope; the modern Mo'orean monarch had electrified the cavern, so perhaps they really were in the right time again. Fask could send them a jet and Raval would be done with trying to make more magic than he was reliably capable of. He was more than ready to pass the torch of adventure on to someone who would enjoy it more.

The lights blinked out and back to brightness, and another pair of lights came on, and then another.

Raval realized with a little shock in his chest that they weren't lights at all.

They were eyes.

Cindy screamed.

CHAPTER 24

The car was surrounded by dragons. There were dozens of them, Katy thought, each of them the size of a city bus. As her eyes grew used to the dim again, she could see them swirling around outside the Firedome, trailing tails and rustling wings, peering in through the windows with eyes like glowing serving platters.

"Friends of yours?" she squeaked at Raval. They were twice or three times as big as Raval, she thought.

Lancelot was barking and lunging at the windows in turn, utterly determined to protect his children at any cost. As long as there was glass between them, at least.

Katy wasn't sure how well the glass would hold up, particularly when one of them tapped claws across the windshield, like a terrible moment from a Jurassic Park movie.

"Can you talk to them?" Katy asked Raval. "Like with your mind or something?" They certainly weren't acting friendly, or offering to shift to their human forms.

"It doesn't work that way," Raval said in that tight way that meant he was thinking really hard. "It would be convenient if we could, believe me. My brothers and I have sort of a body language that we can use when we're flying together, but these are definitely not my brothers. And they don't look like the Mo'orean dragons, either."

One of the dragons knocked bodily into the car with its shoulder, rocking it in place, and all the children shrieked except Randal, who was panting and running his fingers together frantically.

The car fell back onto its tires and Raval reached for his door handle. "Stay back," he warned.

"What are you doing?" Katy asked, trying not to sound as panicked as she felt. "Where are you going?"

"Maybe if I show them that I'm a dragon, they'll shift and we can talk," he said, sounding sensible and completely calm. Katy knew by now that this was Raval at his most stressed, behind a perfect mask of serenity. "Stay back, kids."

Cindy and Danny shrunk back across the bench seat into Katy as Raval opened the door. Katy wanted to stop him, to grab desperately at him, but instead, she focused on getting the children back from the brink of hysteria. She put one arm around Danny and Cindy and reached back over the seat to comfort the kids in the back with the other. Lancelot whined and scrambled over the laps between them to lick her arm. "Stay back," she warned unnecessarily, as Raval slipped out of the door and stepped away from the car, closing the door quickly behind him.

The dragons did draw away slightly, giving Raval just enough room to shift, and when he did, their shock and alarm was obvious; they all mantled back, spreading their wings, hissing, and retreating from the car.

None of them shifted into human forms.

Katy switched places with Cindy and Danny so that she could see out the window better, and they huddled up close behind her and peered around. They had all stopped screaming, but most of them were still sobbing and shocky. It was one thing to have a friendly dragon-Raval to play with. These dragons were bigger, and clearly aggressive. Randal was humming tunelessly and loud. Lancelot was panting and whining, his nose to the glass.

Raval might be a smaller dragon than they were, Katy thought, but he had a stillness and nobility that the others lacked. He was much more nicely formed than they were.

Possibly, she was biased.

He wasn't posturing like they were, snarling and raising the spines along his back, only sitting calmly with his wings folded primly against himself while they circled and snuffled and growled.

One of the stranger dragons bumped the car again, accidentally by Katy's guess, and all the children screamed in fright like they were on an amusement park ride.

That did make Raval sit up taller, spread his wings, and roar a challenge to the offending dragon, who slunk back to the others as if he'd just been chastised.

"Who are you and why are you here?"

All the children gasped and shrank back. Danny and Cindy tried to crawl directly into Katy's armpits.

Katy turned to find that there was a woman sitting in the seat that she'd abandoned, a woman with an oval face who glowed blue around all of her edges and had long dark hair that looked wet but floated around her like it was weightless. Her eyes were the only normal thing about her.

Lancelot tried to lunge over the seat to get to her, but he seemed chiefly to be interested in climbing into her lap and licking her rather than savaging her.

The woman—spirit?—seemed taken aback by the dog's forward friendliness and met him nose-to-nose for a moment of unspoken communication that put him into a stupor. Lancelot sat down with the kids in the back bench seat, blinking happily and leaning into their arms as they trembled and held on to him.

"I'm...Teacher Katy," Katy said, not sure what else to say. She wanted to turn and watch Raval's standoff with the unfriendly dragons, but there was a magic woman in her car, and that required more immediate attention. Raval was smart, and the dragons didn't seem inclined to hurt him. Besides which, Katy wasn't sure what she could personally do against a dozen giant dragons.

Of course, Katy wasn't confident there was much she could do against the glowing woman, should she turn out to be hostile.

"Why have you disturbed our treaty with the dragons?" the woman asked intently. "What is this conveyance you have come in? Why are these men and women smaller? Does the dog also change shapes?"

Katy forced herself to focus on one remarkable question at a time and started with the simplest. "This is a car. An, er, magic car. It's a...mechanical carriage. The small ones were stolen from their homes and we—Raval and I—went to get them back. And that dog does not change shape, though there are some that do. We did not realize that we were crashing your party."

Before Katy could consider that she was speaking in a vernacular that the woman would probably not understand if she didn't recognize a car, Randal asked from the back seat, "Are you an angel?"

None of the other kids giggled or mocked him for the question, though Cindy sucked in her breath and shrank closer to Katy. The woman turned and fixed her uncanny gaze on him without mercy.

But when Katy expected that it might make Randal uncomfortable and, on the heels of what they had just gone through—were still going through!—even precipitate a meltdown, Randal met her stare in kind.

A slow smile spread across her face. "How curious. You may call me Angel," she invited. "Enough of this."

As suddenly as she'd appeared, she was gone, and Katy turned to see that she was standing outside the car by Raval, holding one hand up to the largest dragon that was facing him down. She was so brilliant that Katy could see all the dragons now; there were only about a dozen of them now that they were still, settling into a semi-circle facing Raval.

Raval seemed to startle when he saw the spirit, starting to unfold his wings before he settled them back again.

"You kids stay here," Katy said, peeling Cindy and Danny off of her and reaching for the door handle. If they had been any other children, she would have expected protests, if not outright disobedience, but she knew that they would all do as she said. She wasn't going to leave Raval to face this company alone, and she thought there wasn't much she could do in the car against a spirit who could appear inside the car at will, anyway.

Maybe a united front would be beneficial.

But when she got out, slamming the door behind her so that it would latch, Katy was alarmed to find that the spirit had been joined by more of her kind, standing in a hemisphere facing the dragons.

There were more like twenty of them, representing, as far as Katy could tell, many different races. Some of them looked like they were actively ablaze, their features smearing like she was seeing them behind a bank of heated air. Some of them, like Angel, looked like they were floating underwater. One had leaves instead of hair from their head, and long, twig-like fingers. There were women and men in the mix, and some that defied categorization.

They were so bright that the cave was completely illuminated. For a moment, Katy thought they'd traveled to a new place, then she realized that the cave had the same entrance and the same vaulting ceiling and organic grace, but lacked the carved alcoves for each of the virtues. Had they been removed? Or had the car taken them earlier in time, before they'd been carved?

Katy had a moment of despair, wondering if they would only ever slip backwards in time, to the time of dinosaurs, maybe, or to the big bang? Would God be waiting there?

"What are they saying?" Katy asked Raval as she stepped beside his solid dragon form. She remembered belatedly that he'd said they couldn't speak that way.

He shifted back to his human form, and even in the middle of what was clearly some kind of supernatural stand-off, Katy was distracted by how impossibly good-looking he was. Even without shaving or soap for a few months, he was any straight woman's fantasy. Katy couldn't help but chuckle. Her very own magical, dragon-shifting Alaskan prince. What was the title of this book? The Nanny Swiss Family Dragonson? She suspected that they were more like Gilligan's Island.

Both the spirits and the dragons seemed shocked by Raval's second transformation, drawing back their heads, shuffling in place, and giving a murmur of surprise as they stared at them.

Katy stepped forward and found his hand, twining his fingers into her own. Whatever happened next, they would face it as a team.

"It is tiresome communicating this way," one of the spirits said, and the largest and most central of the dragons seemed to agree, bowing its head and growling. "Will you fix it or must I?"

The dragon lifted his forepaw into the air and gestured with two sharp claws. Lightning sizzled and snapped away in a bubble of light that washed out over everyone before Katy could even freeze up in fear.

She didn't feel any different after it passed through her, but the cavern seemed to swell with voices.

"Is it a dragon or a man? I do not know him."

"Why are there small ones? What are they?"

"Is this a trick of our rivals?"

"This meeting is a grievous mistake."

"We should take what we need, there is no need to treat with these! They lack our magic and our strength."

"Peace!"

That was the first dragon, the one who had cast the magic, and all the others subsided obediently.

Angel and another of the spirits had stepped forward. "Identify yourselves."

Katy thought they were speaking to her and Raval, but it was the largest dragon who answered. "I am First here," they said.

The spirits regarded them with calculation. "You are the one who will answer for the crime of your presence?"

"It is not a crime," one of the other dragons protested. "You have no claim on this world!"

"You have no more right here than we do," one of the spirits said fiercely. "You are not from this place, either."

"Peace," First repeated. "We asked to meet in order to forestall the disruption of this world with our conflict."

"They've *already* disrupted it," a dragon protested. "We should simply wipe them out."

"Regardless of the wrong," Angel said, her voice rising over the rest, "we can all see the future if we stay to this path."

Katy wondered how literally she meant the statement. Could they genuinely see the future?

And rather suddenly, they were all staring at Katy, Raval,

and the car full of children—and one dog—with their noses pressed to the window.

"The strange conveyance has dragged the scent of their future here with them," one of the dragons said in wonder. "I can smell the possibilities that they came through."

"How unexpected," a rock-skinned spirit observed.

"You will destroy the world," First said flatly.

"You will be the fuel," Angel countered.

"This world deserves better," the fire spirit beside her said gently.

"A world in ruins serves none of us." That was a graceful dragon that came to First's side and looked plaintively up at him. As plaintively as a great, lizard-skinned monster could possibly look, Katy thought.

"And so we accepted your invitation to treat," Angel said firmly. "Examine that future yourself."

"There is harmony if we can reach agreement," First agreed. "As far forward as I am able to see."

"There is no *harmony* with such beings," the dragon on his other side protested. "They do not have our power. We can simply stop them, First, we don't have to contract with them."

"Dragons are not *honorable*," one of the spirits argued. "This is a trap to weaken us and wipe us out."

"We cannot trust *a spirit's* word," a dragon countered.

"We can make a contract that binds us both," First said. "If we can concur on terms."

Both parties hissed their distrust of each other.

"We need something of this world to negotiate," Angel said impatiently. "A neutral party we can both agree to."

Katy and Raval were rather suddenly the center of all their attention again.

"That one is a dragon," a smoke-spirit protested. "He is biased!"

"He is not one of us!" a dragon snarled to a murmur of agreement.

Katy had watched fights escalate between children many times, and she recognized the simmering distrust

"I understand," Raval said, unexpectedly. "I understand."

"I don't," Katy squeaked.

CHAPTER 25

*R*aval understood with a burst of clarity that almost hurt, and he wasn't sure it was entirely from his own mind. The first dragon was looking at him, and Raval thought that he might have attempted a form of communication that was beyond the ability of his own mind.

"Neither of you is from here," he said. "This is not your world. You've come from other worlds, worlds of magic."

"They're from fairyland?" Katy murmured beside him.

"Close enough," Raval said, but he was concentrating now, trying to sort out all the things that had bloomed into his brain. He turned to Angel. "I know you. We always thought that you were a natural spirit, but you aren't."

She looked at him in disgust. "I don't know *you*," she protested.

Raval shook his head. "Not now, but in the future."

She looked thoughtful. "I still exist, in your future?"

Raval looked at her and thought he could see her fading at the edges. "This world isn't good for you," he observed, trying to resolve the contradiction. "Not the way you are now."

Angel hissed at him like a feral cat that he'd stepped too close to. "I can make it worse for you," she threatened.

"Don't damage the human," First cautioned. "We will take that as an act of war and cut you down where you stand."

"Of course he'd protect the little human-dragon," one of the spirits whispered in disdain.

Raval looked at First. "And you. You're the first dragon. You wrote the Compact. Will write the Compact. Are writing the Compact?"

"I don't know this Compact of which you speak," First said severely. "But I am left with more questions."

There was a tap on the window of the car behind them. "Can we come out, Teacher Katy?" a thin voice called. One of the kids had found the window crank. Lancelot was trying to stick his nose out of the tiny crack, licking it enthusiastically.

"Explain the small ones," First said. "What are they?"

"They're children," Katy explained. "Just a second, Franky."

The car became the focus of attention in the cave, which Raval actually felt was more disturbing than when they were staring at him. He bristled protectively.

One of the spirits made of smoke blinked out and materialized next to Katy. "She has one *inside* of her!"

This prompted a murmur of surprise and revulsion.

"They *procreate*," a fire spirit said in disgust. "They make small ones out of flesh. That is how they persist with such short lives. I tell you, they are not worth saving."

Raval stepped closer to Katy, but she was gazing at the smoke spirit with what Raval thought was compassion.

"You can't have children, can you."

The smoke spirit vanished, reappearing on the opposite side of the cave as if Katy's words had shaken it.

Raval was confused for a moment, thinking of the child spirit who had haunted the cave while he worked on the car, then blinked in unexpected clarity. It was the Compact, in its early days, before its magic was fully developed by multiple Renewals and iterations of its magic.

"We *persist,*" Angel said. "We do not duplicate. That is a conceit of this world."

"It is a curious quality," First agreed, but he sounded intrigued, not disgusted.

"Curious or not," Katy said firmly, "we will not let you hurt them. I would be very grateful if they could get out and stretch their legs, though. Perhaps have a snack, while you are figuring out how to play nicely with each other. Something, I should note, that *they* have already mastered."

A dragon's laugh was an alarming grunt and a cave full of them would frighten anyone, but Katy didn't waver a moment, standing with her hands easy at her side as she stared down two supernatural forces.

After a moment, Angel also laughed, the sound a tinkle of music. "We will not hurt them."

"The children have our protection," First agreed gravely. "For the time."

"Can I have ice cream?" Lon asked through the crack in the car.

"There's no ice cream here," one of the others chided him.

"There might be!" Lon protested. "We don't know when we are."

"When was ice cream invented?" Danny asked. "Randal?"

"Let us speak alone together," Angel proposed to First. "This taste of the future is not one I had anticipated and I know that you did not, either. We have more to...ponder together now."

"Leave us," First commanded. The dragons flickered out of the cave like they were fading into shimmers of light and after a moment, the spirits followed, leaving only Angel and First, in relative darkness.

Were they making portals? Raval wondered clinically. Magic didn't seem to follow the rules it usually did. Then he laughed dryly. No, the rules of magic hadn't been written yet. On an impulse, he focused his thoughts and drew a glowing orb out of thin air in the palm of his hand. It lit the cave easily.

It would have been handy to have that to work on the car earlier. Later. However time worked when you went backwards through it.

No words. No meditation. No activation. Just chaos. There was something wrong about it, but Raval couldn't put his finger on it, exactly, he only knew that it didn't feel right.

"Can we go to the beach?" Cindy asked impatiently. "If this is going to take a while…"

"We can't go anywhere else right now," Raval said, eyeing the car by the light of his globe. If their first trip had burned out his spell, this one had probably destroyed even more.

"It will be simple to fix," First said, as if he had heard Raval's thoughts. "I can assist you. But first, stay and tell us more of this future that you brought with you. I am intrigued."

"We can go to the beach," Katy said and the children needed no other invitation to pile out of the car. Lancelot's leash was held tightly, so that he couldn't escape, and he whined in protest, tugging to the end of it.

Katy paused as they mobbed cheerfully towards the entrance of the cave, for all the world as if they were just on another field trip. Perhaps, with everything they had gone through and seen, this was not so surprising to them.

"Will you be alright?" Katy asked anxiously.

"We will not harm him," First said thunderously.

Angel rolled her eyes. "Very dramatic. I also agree not to snuff him out yet. His insights to the future he came from may be enlightening."

Katy didn't look terribly reassured and Raval remembered that comforting her was his job. "I'll be fine," he promised. "It's understandable that they have questions. Go keep an eye on the kids…and remember that they'll be magic now. Chaos magic."

"Don't let them draw," Katy said with a wry chuckle as she dropped a swift kiss on his cheek. "This was so not in the job description."

It wasn't until she'd left that Raval realized what was so wrong with the magic he was working. "This magic, it isn't from this world at all." He eyed the dragon and the spirit. "It's from *yours.*"

CHAPTER 26

Katy went with the children to a beach that had been transformed.

"Our tents are gone!"

"The latrine isn't there!"

"The beach is different!"

"Look how little the climbing tree is!"

It was very odd, because they had only been gone perhaps twenty minutes. Twenty very odd minutes, admittedly. It was morning again, though they'd left with evening approaching, and it was cloudy and overcast, not sunny.

"The firepit was here," Paige said, pointing, and very abruptly, it appeared, with a cracking fire already lit within it.

"We're magic!" Cindy remembered, and then there were blazing butterflies taking off from her fingertips.

"Careful," Katy warned, but each of them was already weaving enchantment at the breakneck speed of their imagination, and she wasn't sure what harm they could do.

"We could make a castle!" Prit exclaimed, and a giant wall rose before them with an ornate wooden door.

After a moment of wonder, they went in, to find that it was far smaller than it looked, and completely empty. "I didn't think about what would be inside," Prit confessed.

"We can fill it up," Lon suggested. They each created furniture—long, bulldog couches, a bed with a frilled quilt, easy chairs, stools—until it was so crowded they could barely move.

"What now?" Katy asked, feeling like there was a lesson here.

"Ice cream!" Franky said, and he was holding a bowl heaped with scoops.

That led to a flurry of food requests. Jamie burnt her fingers on a bowl of soup and dropped it to shatter on the floor. It was cleaned up with one quick gesture from Lon while Cindy comforted her.

Katy's stomach rumbled and she wondered wistfully if she could summon her own food. These children had started out magical, but she hadn't.

"Taco," she said, envisioning a plate in her outspread hands. Nothing happened.

"I'll make you tacos," Cindy offered and Katy nearly dropped the platter that appeared in her hands.

Katy tried her best to enjoy them, but they tasted like tacos magicked into being by a person who barely remembered what tacos were. They didn't have quite the right crunch, and they tasted distant and disappointing.

"This isn't really ice cream," Franky said sadly, banishing his sundae. "It isn't quite right."

"I'd rather gather food," Jamie said thoughtfully. "It means more."

"I miss our tents," Lon added.

Prit gave a sigh and snapped his fingers. The castle and all the mismatched furniture vanished. Paige smoothed her firepit back to solid ground.

"I thought it would be more fun if magic was easier," Cindy said thoughtfully. A glowing magical salamander was twining through her fingers and when she shook it off it dissolved into sparks.

"What's going to happen now, Teacher Katy?" Danny wanted to know.

"I don't know," Katy said honestly. She found a piece of driftwood to sit on where the firepit had been. "All of history, I guess? Raval will try to keep history the way that we know it, so we go back to where we were. That means getting the dragons and the spirits to agree to write a binding Compact."

"They didn't like each other," Jamie observed frankly.

"Sometimes, people that don't like each other still have to find a way to agree," Katy said.

"It's easier if you do like each other," Cindy said. "Maybe Raval can *make* them like each other."

Katy had to laugh. "If anyone can, he can," she said with confidence. "But it might take a while and we might need to stay here a few nights. What do we need?"

This was something that the kids willingly tackled, eager to put their hard-won skills to use. Magic made them tents again, rendered in loving detail from their strong memories of the shelter they'd been using the past several months. Some of them struck out with Lancelot to gather fruit and Franky led an expedition to capture fish. They fell into familiar patterns easily, constructing a camp from nothing in a matter of hours.

Paige rebuilt her firepit with rocks and sand, and gathered real wood and tinder, though she lit it with a spark of magic because Raval was not available with dragon fire.

Real food was considerably more satisfying than the magic food had been, even if Katy was wickedly tired of fish.

CHAPTER 27

Raval was the center of all of the attention, from both of these hostile parties, and he didn't enjoy it at all.

"You brought this wild magic here with you," he realized. "The magic that was here before, the magic of ordinary shifters, the little earth magics, it doesn't feel the same. You dragged a different kind of magic here with you from your worlds."

"As you dragged the future you came from with you," Angel said, not disagreeing with his assessment.

"Like rising wet from water," First agreed.

They were like amphibians, Raval thought. They would dry out and die when this slick of magic they'd brought with them faded to nothing. But even he knew better than to liken them to frogs. "Neither of you can live in this world very long without your magic. Not as you are. And it will burn up this world if you fight with it for dominance."

First and Angel were both gazing at him, suspicious, but listening.

"Tell us of the future, little mixed-blood," Angel

commanded. "If we are alive in your future, how do we stay that way?"

Raval was not a diplomat. He was the brother who snuck out of formal events and considered it a win if he didn't embarrass the family. He should not be here, doing this. This was a job for Fask, or for any of his other brothers. Tray would be better at this. Drayger would be better at this. *Lancelot* would be better at this.

But Katy's faith buoyed him, and Raval was keenly aware that the entire future of the world hinged on his ability to get them to do something that had already occurred.

He wasn't sure how he was going to make it happen, but he started by explaining what he knew. "In our early history, the first dragon sacrificed his skin to make the Compact that binds our countries."

"Tell me more of this Compact made from *my skin*," First said. Raval wasn't sure if he was offended or amused—it was hard enough to determine that from people, and dragons were harder still to read.

Can you tell? he asked his dragon.

He is not laughing, his dragon replied with a shrug.

Raval complied with the letter of the request, with nothing else to go on.

"Magic is not widely known in our world. It's a secret. The Compact is officially a trade and protection treaty between a series of countries led by dragon-shifting monarchies."

"It is more than a treaty of words," Angel surmised.

"It is a spell," Raval explained. "The most complicated spell in existence. The most complicated spell in *imagination*. It binds the kingdoms and regulates magic itself in the world."

First lowered his big head and leveled Raval with one of his eyes. "You're suggesting that the Compact is how we survive. It's how you bind the magic into us so that we can survive here."

"It's how *you* bind the magic," Raval corrected. "It was written long before I was born. I am not a caster equal to that task." Was he being pedantic?

"Where do you fit in all of this?" Angel wanted to know. "How are you both man and dragon? Are spirits in your time bound to men as well?"

"You are bound to places," Raval explained. "I know you in the future as the spirit of the waterways of Alaska. You have a hot spring where we see you most."

Angel made a face of disgust. "That is appalling. I won't do it."

"Nor would I share a body with a human," First agreed. "I touched your mind, and it is too full and inflexible to join with."

Then he paused, swinging his head towards the entrance to the cave and gave a thoughtful intake of air. "The children, though! They are not as fully formed as you, and they are more fluid. We could bind ourselves to them."

Raval's first instinct was to deny the possibility with all his soul. They'd come there to protect the children, to save them from being used. How could they simply hand them over now, for some new kind of puppetry?

But...there were eleven of them, from all the different nationalities. Just as there were eleven original members of the Small Kingdoms. He blinked rapidly, trying to settle the possibilities into place. He'd written the spell on the car with careful consideration of time causality—was this part of its purpose? Had he unwittingly brought the children from Amara's clutches to where they were actually meant to be, here in the past?

Was it *right*?

The moral implications staggered him.

"I'm not offering you the children," he said firmly. "They aren't possessions to be traded in a negotiation. If that's the path you choose, you must convince them yourselves."

"That is not a choice," Angel scoffed. "I would never bond with such monsters."

First tilted his head, fixing her with one glowing eye. "We would not do it without assurance that the fae will also bind to the world as it is shown in your future."

"I would rather burn this world with us," Angel said with casual indifference.

Raval wasn't sure if it was bluster. Something suggested to him that she was bluffing. Was it only because he trusted the future that he knew?

"I will consult with my people," First said. "Your flesh tires and requires rest, so we will recess for now and meet again a time later."

Raval backed away to the car and sat down on the hood, not sure how much longer he could have stood.

"You know me."

Angel's voice near his ear opposite to where she'd been made him swing around with a crackle of instinctive magic at his fingertips.

Angel gestured and snuffed out the lightning he'd been holding with no effort. Raval *missed* the rules of magic. He'd never had to worry about accidentally lighting someone on fire before. What if it had been one of the children who had startled him?

"You know me in the future," she said, coming to sit on the hood of the car beside him.

Raval was a tangle of worries. He feared that he had failed in negotiating. He'd failed Katy. He couldn't protect his mate, he couldn't protect their baby. He didn't know what would happen to the children if they didn't want to be dragons. Would the dragons try to force them if they decided that was their destiny? What if the fae didn't agree to their terms? He didn't have a shred of diplomacy left in him.

"I wouldn't call us friends," Raval said. "You're a pain in the ass in that time, too."

Angel smirked, then sobered. "But...I'm *alive*. We all are."

Raval shrugged. "I think so. You once said that some of your kind slept." That reminded him of something, and Raval filed the thought to pursue later, when he'd solved the problems already before him.

"The fae world we came from is much different than this one," Angel observed, trailing her fingers over a line of words that had been scratched out. "It burned with endless power, and the magic was louder and brighter. This world has magic of its own, but the only beings who use it at all are the shapeshifters. It seems wasted. I thought...I thought when we came here that we could control it, but the truth is that our power is waning here. We cannot tap into it. Not this way."

Raval had a stab of hope. "You cannot tap it unless you are a *part* of it," he suggested.

"Without binding to the world, we have only shreds of power. Scraps. But I do not wish to be *bound*."

"It beats the alternative," Raval pointed out. "You *could* war with the dragons."

Angel was quiet, and he knew that she was considering the implications. "The dragons still have an anchor of power to their own world. If we could do such a thing..." She shook her head. "They did not leave their world as we did." Her voice was complicated. Sorrowful? Angry? Raval didn't have enough data to know.

"If we agreed to bind to these places, we can *endure*," she said firmly. "We will not wither away, we will not fade. And we will be a part of the world as long as the Compact is intact."

"That is my understanding," Raval agreed.

"We are oil here, to this world's water," Angel observed. "If we live as we are in this place, our own magic will always be in *conflict* with the natural order and it will eventually kill us. We left our world to escape war. I do not relish a finite lifetime more of it. If the dragons bind with men, they will diminish and become a part of this world as we would; they will not triumph over us."

"They would not win," Raval said, thinking about the games his brothers played. "But you would not, either."

"A stalemate," Angel said thoughtfully. She exhaled a cloud of fog. "I don't particularly like it," she admitted, "but I don't have a better solution. "

"Sometimes, the best you can do is the best you can do," Raval said knowingly. "I can't promise that this is the only or easiest path forward. All I can do is tell you that I know the future that it leads to, and it's a good future."

"Is it?" Angel said shrewdly.

"It isn't free of flaws and failing," Raval conceded. He thought about how complex life could be, full of loss and longing. And he thought about his baby with Katy, about his brothers and all the beautiful things that had been created in the times between then and now. "But it has hope and love. That is better than a world that is razed to nothing."

Angel was quiet so long that Raval thought his words had been in vain.

"Perhaps that is enough." Then she vanished.

CHAPTER 28

Katy didn't need a mate bond to know that Raval was agitated as he strode towards her down the trail to the cave.

He looked wild around the eyes and his shoulders were rolled up tensely.

She stood up too fast and got light-headed, but powered through to meet him and pretend that nothing was wrong. She wasn't sure if it was the heat, her spirit-confirmed pregnancy, or the sheer surreality of everything that was happening. "How is it going? Have you convinced them to write the Compact and send us back to our own time?"

Raval glanced at the children, then led Katy away down the shore. She was having them doing sums in the wet sand by the lagoon, challenging each other with multiplication and division, trying to maintain the level of normalcy that they'd found in the last time they lived.

"What is it?" she asked, concerned by his unease.

"The dragons want the children."

"For what?" Katy demanded. The first thing that she thought of was eating them—she hadn't ever seen them actually consuming anything, but legends of dragons did come with voracious appetites.

"They want to bond with the children and set them as the first rulers of the Small Kingdoms to write the Compact," Raval said flatly.

Katy opened her mouth and then closed it. She had to do it again a few times before she could form words again. "They would be the first kings and queens of the Kingdoms," she said in astonishment. "*They* are the magicians who will *cast* the Compact." That was better than the dragons *eating* them, she supposed.

"I told them that the kids had to make the choice," Raval clarified. "I couldn't choose something that big for them."

"That's big," Katy agreed, still feeling like she was in shock. "Dragon big. Destiny big." She chuckled weakly. "How did I not see it?" she asked in wonder. "There are *eleven* of them. Of all different kingdoms."

"How are we supposed to ask these kids to make a choice like this?" Raval wanted to know. "We'd have to leave them here. In the past. We promised to take them *home*. We were supposed to find them families, not chain them to thrones."

Katy was still wrestling with all the implications and complications herself. "They'd be dragons. Kings and queens. Figures of history." Her light-headedness was not really ebbing. "Maybe this *is* the home we promised them. When do the dragons need their answer?"

Raval shrugged. "They don't really have a sense of time passing like we do."

Katy sighed. "I don't see a reason to wait. Let me tell them. You look exhausted, go rest."

"I'll go see if I can help the dragons fix the car," Raval countered, because he, like Katy, wasn't all that good at resting. "They probably don't know how alternators work."

Katy looked at each of the children as she went to

gather them around the fire, sharing their day's exploits so far and trying to best each other in their favorite games. She tried to imagine each of them grown up, with crowns heavy on their brows. It was a burden she had already had to face, but with four other mates, hers was only a possibility, not a sure destiny. For them, was it already a matter of history?

What did that even do to the idea of self-determination?

"Are you okay, Teacher Katy?" Jamie sat beside her and cuddled up close. There was a hint of rain in the air; it was cooler that afternoon than it often was and the fire was a welcome source of warmth.

"I have some news for you," she said calmly. "Gather everyone up by the fire."

"Hey!" Jamie hollered, right next to Katy's ear. "Hey! Come here, everyone! Teacher Katy's got something to say!"

Katy was patient while they all did their usual deferral of what they all thought was an unwelcome task or another lesson.

"Just a second!"

"Let me just finish..."

"I'm almost done with this."

Katy watched them as they dawdled and delayed and dragged their feet, smiling sadly at the behavior that she would have given her heart to see when they'd all just met. They had changed so *much* from the shy, self-contained children that had been freed from Amara's grasp. They had explored their autonomy on the island, and packed a lifetime of childhood into a few short months.

Would she be handing them over to a new kind of control? Or was she setting them free? Had she prepared them well enough and taught them the right things in the short time that they'd had?

Eventually, they all gathered close, sitting on their driftwood stumps or flexibly in the sand with the enviable carelessness of youth.

"Shh," Cindy commanded. "Teacher Katy has to tell us something."

"Shh, yourself," Lon scoffed.

"Shh!"

Katy waited until they were all quiet and watching her.

"You kids have been through so much. No children should have to do what you did for Amara. And we ended up lost on Mo'orea and we had to rely on each other like grown ups, even though you weren't grown ups. I am so proud of your strength and your flexibility, of your willingness to work, and your support of one another."

She looked around at each of them, all of them almost supernaturally still now, gazing at her with every ounce of their attention. "No one has really asked you what you want of your lives. You are smart and insightful and you have big hearts, and you've always had each other. What do you want next in your lives?"

They stared at her for so long that Katy worried she had left the question too open-ended. How, exactly, did you ask children—however old they might be inside after Amara's meddling—to take on the impossible weight of a crown? To say nothing of a dragon that would be melded to their soul.

"I want to be a cook," Franky said shyly.

"I want to be an artist!" Danny exclaimed.

"An acrobat!"

"A pilot!"

"Famous!"

"A kitty cat!" Jamie said.

"That's not a thing you can be," Cindy scoffed.

"She didn't give us any boundary conditions," Jamie protested. They had been talking about scientific method and closed and open systems.

"It's not a rhetorical question," Katy said, when they looked at her for clarification. "Do you remember what rhetorical means?"

"It means you don't expect an answer," Paige volunteered. "So that means, you do?"

"I want to be a hero," Cindy said promptly.

"Yeah, who wouldn't?" Prit said with a shrug.

Katy swallowed. "You kids have the chance to do something really important. But no one is going to make you do it, you would have to choose to do it."

She had all of their attention now, and they had that uncanny stillness that they'd had when she first met them. No one was fidgeting or playing with the sand or poking the fire. No one was being dramatic or whispering with their neighbor.

She looked at Randal. "Do you remember the names of all the first kings and queens of the Small Kingdoms?"

He looked pleased to be the focus of her attention, nodded more vigorously than necessary, and started to rattle them off. "Ladranyikayer of Alaska, Yadanilerolik of Majorca, Rilleressicanica of New Siberian islands..."

Katy let him go through once, then prompted him to list them again, pointing at each of the children in turn.

He got halfway through the list before they realized the significance. From any other group of children, Katy would have expected amazement and excitement, perhaps some emotional acting out. Definitely some outburst.

Instead, they reached for each others' hands, almost simultaneously, and clasped each other in support.

Randal was the last to realize what she was implying and when he turned in confusion to Jamie, who was sitting beside him, she gently told him, "You'll be the king of Alaska."

"If you want," Katy added quickly. "The dragons won't force you."

"Wait," Danny said. "Wait! We're going to *be* dragons?"

"They will bond with you, if you choose it," Katy explained. "Like Raval is with his dragon. You'd share one body and be able to shift between two forms like he can."

Their eyes went to saucers and several of them sighed in joy. A few looked frightened.

Katy waited, but they did not turn to her with questions, only to each other.

"We'd be kings and queens," Jamie whispered. "Of all the Small Kingdoms."

"Can we *do* that?"

"I thought we were trying *not* to mess up the timeline," Franky protested.

Randal was very, very quiet.

"When do we have to decide?" Cindy asked thoughtfully.

"They're waiting for your answer now," Katy said. "But you can take as much time as you need to think about it. Sleep overnight on it if you want, talk about it, whatever you need."

They whispered together for some time and Katy knelt to tend to the sputtering fire and give them a little space.

When she rose again, her back complaining, the children were all standing.

"We don't have to think about it anymore," Cindy said decisively. "We're ready now."

* * *

THE DRAGONS WERE WAITING for them at the beach, a loose semicircle of them across the sand with the ocean at their backs. This gave the children a little elevation as they approached, but they were still intimidating, towering creatures and the kids looked very small and helpless confronting them. Katy was glad to have Raval at her side again.

"You have been told of the solution you pose?" First said. "You come of your own will to be bound to us and to rule the first kingdoms of this world?"

Cindy, facing him boldly, crossed her arms. "No."

CHAPTER 29

Raval heard Katy give a little gasp of shock as Cindy fearlessly faced down the giant monster but he smiled at the little girl's bold answer. Somehow, it didn't surprise him.

He was quite sure by now that these children were not entirely the age that their bodies said they were, changed and made flexible by their unorthodox upbringing. Katy had told him Mackenzie's theory that they had already lived a non-linear amount of time, and that matched Raval's admittedly limited understanding of children.

First lowered his head to Cindy and angled to stare at her with one big eye, but she didn't flinch at his proximity. "What do you mean, no? How is this offer not in any way to your pleasure and the preservation of history?"

Cindy puzzled over his wording for a moment, then said firmly, "It's not fair."

"Not fair to you, puny human child?" First said in outrage. "You would have our power and our guidance and rule the very world."

"It's not fair to the people who are already here," Cindy

insisted. "You can't just plop us down in the middle of a country and say hey, I'm your new king because I'm big and strong and breathe fire."

A few of the kids giggled. Jin pretended to breathe fire.

"We should live with them first and figure out what they need," Paige agreed. "It's like crashing in on a game before you know what the rules are. Winning doesn't necessarily make you fun to play with."

Raval smiled to hear Katy's words from her lips.

First looked back at the other dragons, then again at the children in a loose semicircle before him. They looked very small and fragile in front of the creatures. He cocked his head. "You would separate, and go to each of these kingdoms alone, now? After all your talk of not wanting to be apart?"

"We'll still have each other," Prit explained. "If we're dragons, we can fly and see each other, and talk to each other and help each other out."

"We're still magic," Paige reminded them. "We could make talking rings and magic mirrors."

Raval glanced at Paige sharply, wondering if she knew about Leinani's heirloom rings, or if she'd just come up with them on the spot.

"We have to grow up before we can be kings and queens," Cindy said bravely. "We're just kids right now, and we'll still be kids even with dragons inside of us. But we should grow up in the kingdoms we'll rule, and *earn* our crowns, as part of those kingdoms."

"And not just with strength," Lon added. "With smarts."

Randal was still quietly reciting the names of the first kings and queens.

"We're from the future," Cindy pointed out. "We know more than other people in this time, about science and hygiene and fractions and stuff. We can teach them, and they can teach *us*, and we can grow up and save the world the right way for *everyone*."

"I want it to be fair," Danny said stubbornly.

"It will be *fair*," Cindy insisted. "We'll *make* it fair."

First considered their words. "We could not merge with you when you are grown, so we could not wait for you to mature before we bonded with you."

Cindy fearlessly put her hand out on First's nose. "It's okay," she promised him. "We could teach you, too."

"And we will protect you," First vowed, closing his glowing eyes. "Together, we will save the world and bring it to a just future."

CHAPTER 30

Katy thought with amusement that it looked like nothing so much as a speed-dating session on the beach. Each child spent a short time talking with each of the dragons, solemnly conversing about their favorite pastimes and shyly opening up to see who might be a good match. Lancelot romped between each of them, inserting himself between them and licking all the dragon noses he could reach. The dragons tolerated his exuberance with the same lofty serenity with which they faced everything.

Some of the pairs sorted themselves immediately; Franky and his dragon struck up a conversation about food that was so mutually satisfying that they simply refused to move on to anyone else after they met up on the second swap and started talking.

Cindy gravely spoke with each dragon once and returned to First to announce that they clearly suited each other best because they were both bossy, which he accepted without reservation.

The rest were still bouncing around, narrowing their

choices, when Katy retreated to find a more comfortable seat away from the baking heat of the beach. While she didn't feel particularly pregnant yet, all of her joints ached and she wearied easily of any single position. She worried that she was too restless to sleep next to, but Raval hadn't said a word of complaint.

He looked up when she approached their tent. "I'm getting the car packed up for tomorrow," he said. "The dragons say that it should be able to get us back to our time in one trip with the changes they can make, and we can leave as soon as the ceremony is complete and the kids are off to their new lives."

Tears sprang to Katy's eyes. Was being pregnant making her sensitive and hormonal or was this an appropriate reaction to the news? It wasn't like this was a surprise; it was the next logical step, there was no reason to linger or feel bad now, but Katy couldn't stop the awful tightness in her chest.

Raval looked horrified. "I'm so sorry," he said, opening his arms and scooping her up into an embrace. "We can stay here if you want."

Katy laughed, not sure if he meant it as a joke, or if it mattered that he did. She sobbed and chortled into his big, strong shoulder and let him rock her until she could pull herself together and draw away. "You were amazing," she told him, wiping her eyes. "No one else could have made this work."

"What did I do?" Raval protested. "It's the kids that are taking the biggest risk."

Katy drew in a deep, steadying breath. "You got the fae spirits and the dragons to agree to a binding Compact that diminished them both and saved our world. You found a solution for an impossible situation."

Raval shrugged off her praise. "Honestly, they wanted to agree. No one wants a blistering magical war that destroys their world of refuge. And with the whole causality question, I'm really only a tiny cog in a big machine. All I did was tell them how to do what they already did."

"Give yourself some credit, Raval," Katy scolded him. "*You're* the one who set into motion an entire magical system, a sweeping alliance of kingdoms, our world's whole *history*. You are allowed to take credit for your accomplishments. You are a smart, sexy genius and I love you so much."

She expected him to protest, because she had quickly found that he was not the type to understand his own importance about anything, but she wasn't prepared for the way his whole body stiffened in her arms. "What is it?" she asked, drawing away so that she could see his face. It didn't really give her any clues, but there was a tension in his jaw and neck that she might not have recognized if she didn't know him so well now. "Tell me what's wrong."

"What if I don't *love* you?" Raval said, his voice strangled. "What if I can't?"

Katy gazed at him in consternation, but he wouldn't meet her eyes.

"Why does that worry you?" she asked. Was this the undercurrent of doubt that she'd always felt from him, that tiny thread of misgiving?

"What if I don't know how to love?" he said quietly. "I'm not like other people. I'm shallow. I don't *have* deep emotions. What if I can't be what you need without the matebond to tell me what to do?"

Katy took his face in her hands and kissed his forehead, then wrapped her arms around him to draw him down into her lap. "You forget that I've been able to feel you, too," she reminded him. "I know exactly how deep you run. Just because you aren't good at cues, including your own, that doesn't mean you don't have emotions. You spent more than a decade building a car to save your mother after she died.

You have risked your life to save a classroom full of kidnapped children—twice now! You are loyal to your brothers. You are patient with Lancelot. You are kind and unselfish and honest and you strive to make the people around you happy. What is love if it is not all of that?"

"Duty?" Raval guessed into her cleavage. "Honor? It's what...felt right."

"Love is nothing more than honoring your heart," Katy told him, laying another kiss on the top of his head.

She could feel him relaxing slowly in her arms, gradually turning from stone to warm flesh.

"I love you," Katy said. "You don't have to have a magical connection to know that I do, because I will remind you of it every day, and I will tell you what I am feeling so that you don't have to guess."

"But you won't know what *I'm* feeling," Raval protested. His arms were holding her tight, and he was curled desperately around her.

"You can tell me, if you want," Katy assured him. "But I've seen into your soul, Raval, and you are a beautiful, honorable man who is full of love that you never knew the name for. I will always trust that you care for me and will do what you believe is right."

He didn't answer that, but he did tip his head up and kiss her, slowly and gently. "I love you," he said, as if he was testing the taste of it in his mouth. Then, more firmly, "I love you."

It thrilled Katy to the marrow of her bones, and it lit her on fire to the core of her belly. He'd never been able to *say* it before. "I love you, too."

They undressed each other carefully in their little lean-to tent; it was their only change of clothing and it had become worn in the days they had been trapped in the past. They knew exactly how much pressure each button took to release, slowly slipping shirts off shoulders to spare the seams too much stress.

"Raval," she breathed, when he was touching her knowingly, caressing her clit with one firm finger and pulling her close against his hard cock with his other hand.

"I love you," he said again, and if she hadn't been wet before, she certainly was now; his finger slipping into her was thoroughly lubricated. He worked her to a fever pitch, so intimately familiar with her body and what she liked that they didn't have to pause and ask directions.

"I love you," she agreed, as he laid her down on their primitive bed and spread her legs.

Then he was buried inside of her where he belonged, and they were moving together in that delicious harmony they made, perfectly pitched to each other.

She knew that even if he couldn't feel her pleasure directly, he could feel it in the way she arched beneath him and clawed his back and met him stroke for stroke, and she didn't need his release in her mind to enjoy it with him, the gasping liberation of his need unleashing them both at last.

They had to scramble for their clothing a short time later when they heard a voice calling from just outside their tent. "Teacher Katy? Mr. Prince Raval?" It was Lon.

"Just a minute!" Katy squeaked. She'd enjoy having real walls and doors that latched again in their own time.

Lon was wringing his hands in distress when they emerged, still pulling their clothing into place. "Randal doesn't want to be a dragon!"

CHAPTER 31

There, his dragon said, spotting Randal before Raval noticed him.

Randal was sitting at the end of the beach, rocking and looking out over the ripples that were starting to reflect sunset.

Raval landed and shifted to crouch beside him in the hardened sand. For a long time, they just sat together. Raval hated it when people rushed him; he wasn't going to push Randal.

It was a calm evening, the waves breaking out over the reef far away and there was just enough of a breeze to lift Raval's hair and remind him that it had been entirely too long since he'd gotten a haircut. He wondered if he could magic himself up a pair of scissors. Maybe he could just tell his hair to trim itself. Tray had once cut his own hair, and it had been such a disaster that Mrs. James had to shave his head. He'd probably manage to do something like that if he tried.

Randal was running his fingers together, with the same

motion over and over again. Raval let the sound of the riffly little waves soothe him in the same way.

"I can't do it," Randal finally said, his voice flat and firm. "I'm not like them. I can't do it."

Thanks to Katy, to Katy loving him, Raval had an answer for that. "You don't *have* to be like other people. You are exactly who and what you are and that's all you have to be to be a good king. You're going to be the first king of Alaska, and they are going to write history books about how amazing and forward-thinking you were."

"Is it cheating?" Randal wanted to know. "Because I already know how it's going to be?"

Raval respected his desire for things to be fair, even if experience was likely to teach him that life very rarely was. "Knowing how it will end up doesn't really change the fact that there are a million little decisions that might get there differently," he decided. "You'll have to do a lot of your own work."

If anything, that seemed to reassure Randal.

They sat in silence a little longer, the sound of the gentle surf and Randal's stimming making a harmony that Raval didn't find unpleasant.

"Do you know what this means?" Raval asked at last.

Randal shot him a suspicious look. "That time travel is possible as long as you address causality issues, but really you shouldn't let many people know that, because it could be a huge mess and I'm not sure if the flexibility is infinite."

Raval blinked. "Well...yes, I suppose that's true. But that's not what I was thinking. I just realized that this means you're my great great great-something grandfather."

Randal gave a bark of laughter, and then another. "Okay, sonny," he laughed, and he repeated the joke several times. "Sonny! Grandson! Grandsonny!"

When Randal's mirth had faded into calmer rocking, Raval went on.

"Different isn't less," he said, and he had to bow his head at the truth of his own words. "Different might be harder, but it's important. This is who you are. And you can be the king of Alaska. Just like I can."

Randal nodded slowly.

"You'll have friends, people you trust, who can guide you to understanding how other people think, how to act. You'll have a dragon. Trust him. Have faith. In them, and in yourself."

They returned down the beach to where the other children were still speaking with their dragons, asking all the questions that they could come up with. It was a lot of questions, Raval knew from being on the receiving end of them often enough.

Randal's steps slowed as they approached. Did he worry that he'd gotten the last, unwanted dragon, like a boy being chosen last in sports?

He needn't have fretted. Danny came running to meet them. Danny ran everywhere to make up for the fact that his legs were still the shortest. "Randal, we found the perfect dragon for you! He likes history as much as you do, and he thinks it's too hot here, and he's never heard of skiing!"

Raval let the two return to the dragons with the others, then struck up the slight rise to where their camp was, marveling at the comforting sight of it.

CHAPTER 32

Katy gathered all of the kids on the beach that night around the bonfire that Raval lit when he returned with Randal. She was tired and would have preferred to slip away early when Raval came back, but she knew that they were—ironically—running out of time.

"We're going to be dragons!" Paige was spinning in circles, her arms out, and she was a danger to anyone standing close by.

"Will it hurt?"

"Do I still have to go to bed on time?"

"We could light our own fires, we wouldn't need matches."

"What about Mackenzie?"

"I miss Mackenzie."

Katy let them talk freely at first, speculating about life as a dragon, as the leader of a kingdom, joking about the rules they'd make regarding bedtimes and sweets. Danny snuggled up on one side of her, warm against her side.

Eventually, she started leading the conversation, asking pointed questions about how they would rule, what was fair, who to trust. They all sat down close together. "Which of the six virtues is most important as a king or queen?"

"Strength," Jin said promptly. "You have to be able to protect your kingdom from enemies."

"Courage," Prit said firmly. "Even when you're afraid of stuff, you have to be able to do the right things."

"Loyalty," Franky said thoughtfully. But he shrugged when Katy pressed him for a reason. "It just is," he said stubbornly.

"Patience," Paige insisted. "Otherwise, you'll just get mad all the time and make stupid choices."

"Truth," Danny said. "You can't lie to people or they won't trust you."

Jessica just nodded about everything. Randal changed his mind several times.

It was Cindy who finally said, "I think it's kindness." Jin started to scoff but subsided when she held up a hand to go on. "We're all just people, even if we're dragons too," she explained. "And you can't be strong or loyal without friends. But no one wants a friend who isn't nice. Honesty is important, but if it's mean, it does more harm than good. And kindness makes you patient, because you *care* enough to do things that take time."

They all looked at Katy, to see if Cindy was right, and she smiled and hoped that they couldn't see the tears that were welling in her eyes. *Stupid pregnancy hormones.* "There isn't a right answer," she told them gently. "They're *all* the right answers. There's a reason that there are six virtues and not just one."

The kids seemed mostly satisfied with that conclusion and Katy let the conversation wander for a while before she got to her feet. "I'm beat," she admitted. "Make sure the fire is out before you turn in."

THE DRAGON PRINCE'S MAGIC

"We don't have to go to bed first?" Paige asked in astonishment.

"You're going to be the first kings and queens," Katy pointed out. "I think you can decide when to go to sleep now. You're the ones who will have to deal with the consequences tomorrow."

She left them negotiating over who got to put the fire out and was happy to hear them making the sensible decision to go to sleep *soon*. She wasn't sure if they had the maturity to make *soon* a concrete time, but they would have to learn about that, eventually. That wasn't a thing she could just teach.

The sound of their conversation ebbed away into the evening sounds of the island as she walked up the shore, fading entirely to the distant sound of the ocean and the hum of the insects, occasionally pierced by night birds. Lancelot trotted with her halfway and then decided to turn back. Katy wondered who he'd sleep with that night—it was always a badge of honor among the kids. She and Raval had already decided to take him back to Alaska with them; Lancelot wouldn't enjoy the flight it would require to get to Alaska in this time and he'd be happier home where his fur coat was an asset. Katy was very fond of him by now and wondered if she could get special inside-dog privileges like Tania and Carina had.

Raval had his tools spread out on the table by their little lean-to and he was dumping sand out of the box by the light of an oil lamp. He looked up at Katy's approach. "I don't understand how sand gets into everything," he complained. "I never even had this at the beach."

He answered Katy's kiss with one of his own. He'd gotten easier with casual touches. "How are the kids holding up?" he asked.

"They're good kids," Katy said confidently. "And I would

have faith that they'll be good rulers, even if I didn't have history to tell me that they already were. I'm...going to be sad to leave them." Dammit, there were the tears again.

Raval immediately put down his wrenches and gathered her up into his arms to hold her tight. He was warm and burly and Katy felt utterly safe against him. "We don't have to leave them here," he told her. "Screw history! The dragons say they've fixed the car. We can just pile them all into it with the dog and leave."

Katy leaned her head against him and laughed weakly. "The world needs them here, now," she said softly. "I couldn't be so selfish."

"We could stay here—now—with them," Raval offered reluctantly.

"I want to go home," Katy said plaintively, feeling guilty for the choice. "I want to see my sister again. I want to eat something other than fish."

There were no easy answers, but there were easy kisses after that, and Katy wasn't so tired that she wasn't willing to enjoy a quick, athletic round of sex in the precious privacy that they had.

Pregnancy sex was exquisite, and Katy thought that all of her senses were sharper, and all of her pleasure more keen. Every touch, every caress, felt more intense and meaningful. When he brought her to her final crest of release, she found that she didn't even miss the mate bond, and she felt closer to Raval than ever, like they were more connected than magic could even imagine.

Afterwards, Raval drowsed, but Katy was weirdly awake considering how tired she felt. After a while, she slipped out of his embrace and walked back to the beach.

The fire had been thoroughly quenched, and the children were whispering quietly together in their tents. Katy walked further down the wet sand, both restless and tired, until she got to the place that their elaborate driftwood bench had been in the future. There wasn't anything there now, and the shape of the beach and the bay was slightly different. The sand varied with every tide. Katy sat down in the shifting sand and looked out over the rippling water. Moonlight cast sharp shadows from every tree and half-buried shell.

She looked up in time to see a curious smudge of light in the sky above, growing larger, and then there was a dragon landing on the beach beside her.

How much had her life changed that this seemed perfectly normal?

It was First, and he folded his wings along his back and settled down on his haunches. He still towered over Katy, but she appreciated that he was clearly trying not to loom.

"Are the children prepared for tomorrow?"

"As prepared as they could possibly be," Katy said, bracing herself for tears. They didn't come this time, because whatever else pregnancy was, it was fickle. "Promise me that they'll be okay?" She desperately wanted reassurance that this was the right thing.

"You are the one from the future," First pointed out.

"History doesn't get everything right," Katy countered.

"Hopefully, it gets *enough* right," First said with a chuckle. He went on more soberly. "I am invested in making this equitable for everyone, and for the best and most peaceful future. No one wants war. We care for this world, and respect its original people. The path you propose seems a fitting sacrifice for lasting harmony in a world that is not our own by right."

Kindness, Katy thought, remembering Cindy's words.

"Thank you," she said.

First angled his big head to stare at her with one eye. "What is your thanks for, exactly?"

"For caring," Katy said honestly. "You are powerful beings

from a world of magic. You could have taken what you wanted without trying to fit in. You could have left this world to the fae. You could have fought them to the destruction of the world. You could have forced the children to suit you instead of giving them the option to accept you."

"But apparently, we did not." First did not seem to have any problem at all with fixed futures or self-determination. In some ways, the dragons were totally alien. In other ways, they were almost human.

"You are weary," he observed.

She was, Katy realized. She was tired, but full of hope. The surprise of their solution was starting to settle into what felt right, and her body's exhaustion was catching up with her with a vengeance.

First offered his claw to help her up and she accepted it.

"Thank you," he said.

"What is your thanks for, exactly?" Katy asked, half-teasing.

"For showing us your heart," First said gravely. "For demonstrating the love that your people are capable of. You have been selfless and brave."

Ah, there were the tears again. Katy let her breath out slowly and blinked them back. "I appreciate that," she said simply. "Good night."

The walk back to their tent was a long one and Katy was glad to crawl back into their bed with Raval to sleep. Tomorrow, everything changed. Tomorrow, all of her charges would be bonded to dragons, the Compact itself would be put into motion, and they would go home, to their own time, at last.

CHAPTER 33

There were lights floating all over the cavern, brilliant orbs in all colors illuminating the semi-circular cave. The fresh-carved alcoves had crisp lettering and sharp edges.

"I'm afraid," Jessica confessed to Katy, slipping a hand into hers. "I don't know if I'll *like* being a dragon."

"It's okay to be uncertain or afraid, but I think it sounds amazing," Katy reassured her. All of the kids were agitated, milling around. The dragons had created new clothing for them, and they all wore soft-belted white shirts that fell to their knees. They were all shaggy-haired, boys and girls alike, and they had flower crowns on their heads. It was strange to see them in something other than their familiar, worn pajamas.

She and Raval had been dressed in light, whispery robes. "What is this even made of?" Katy wanted to know, when they transformed her stained and mended shirt and jeans. She didn't think she would miss her old clothing, which had started to get nearly transparent, but after a few months of nothing else to wear, it felt very odd. "Silk? Fairy wings? Dreams?"

Raval was more interested in the etched piece of glass that First had given to him. "A gift of truth," the dragon said, dropping it into his hands. "It will give you answers about your father and it should satisfy the new rules of magic, as will your car."

"I'm your grandfather, Sonny," Randal said, still nearly hysterically amused by the fact. He was stimming, but the other kids were taking turns distracting and comforting him when it looked like things might get overwhelming.

Would Randal *change*, with a dragon in him? Katy had to wonder. Would Cindy? Would they all be the same children? Or would the force of the dragons overwhelm the children altogether, despite the dragons' assurance that it wouldn't?

"They are strong," First told her, as if he could pick the thoughts from the air. Maybe he could. These dragons were bigger and more magical than any in Katy's time. Not that her experience of dragons was truly that broad. "They are uniquely suited to share our minds."

Uniquely suited. Katy wondered if their terrible time with Amara had shaped them into exactly the vessels that were needed. They had experiences—casting magic, witnessing politics and power plays, finding family—that no other children could have had. Amara's magic stone might have even played a role, altering their very minds so that they were able to accept their dragon partners.

It was an unsettling loop, and it was strangely comforting.

"We are ready to begin," Angel called.

The dragons settled themselves in a semi circle before the alcoves they had carved for truth, courage, and kindness. The fae spirits ranged before the other three, strength, patience, and loyalty. The children clustered with Katy briefly, then boldly strode out to meet their chosen dragons.

Before Katy could identify the feelings choking her, she felt Raval's hand slip into hers. "There, there," he said, with a sly sideways look.

"Are you trying to comfort me?" she asked, smiling despite the turmoil inside of her.

"You're probably scared," he offered.

"Scared. Nervous. Excited. Awestruck. This is a lot."

"It's a lot," Raval agreed. "But everything we face, good or bad, we'll face it together. Forever."

The dragons and the children and spirits and huge solemn moment that they were witnessing seemed to fade into the background. Raval was Katy's ground and her center, her everything at once, and knowing that he was here at her side made everything make sense again.

She leaned into him, shoulder against his side as he put his arm around her and they faced the ceremony unfolding before them.

"I take you for my own," First said, gazing down into Cindy's upturned face. Behind him, the other dragons murmured a heartfelt chorus. "For a better future and a lasting peace, I bond with you in this time and the next."

"I take you for my own," Cindy replied, her high voice without a trace of hesitation. "For a better future and a lasting peace, I bond with you in this time and the next." The rest of the children echoed her.

The cave itself was humming. First raised glowing eyes to the spirits that faced him and waited.

Angel stepped forward. "I take this world for my own," she said slowly. "For a better future and a lasting peace, I bond with it in this time."

The air got thicker and hotter, and Katy didn't think that it was just the tension in her own throat or the feeling of Raval's arm tightening around her.

Each of the spirits stepped forward to repeat Angel's

words and seemed to vanish, sinking down into the earth or up into the air, dissolving into ash and mist and smoke as the dragons shimmered in place and faded away altogether. Beneath them, the earth gave a great shudder and Katy heard thunder rumble outside the cave.

The glowing orbs of light winked out abruptly with the sound of a wail like an infant and they were standing in darkness.

"I can't see anything!" Jamie complained, sounding very much like herself.

Raval's arms retreated from Katy and she felt him fumbling in his pocket to find his flashlight and turn it on.

The children looked no different than they had, but they were dressed again in their well-worn pajamas, and Cindy was holding a heaping pile of parchment. They were still wearing crowns of flowers, because those hadn't been magical. Katy was wearing rags again, too.

"Is that…"

Cindy looked down at it. "This is the Compact. It was… like he pulled the rules from my head and wrote them down."

Raval's face scrunched up. It had more lines than usual in the stark light of the flashlight, like he was suddenly older. "It was supposed to take decades to write."

"The first dragon was also supposed to sacrifice his skin to write it on," Katy observed. "Though I suppose in some ways that he did."

"I have a dragon," Cindy said, her voice full of wonder. "I'm not alone."

"It's like I'm huger on the inside of my head!" Lon exclaimed.

Katy was crying again, curse her hormones, and the kids all danced around and hugged each other and came to embrace her and give Raval tackle-hugs.

"The tents are gone!" Lon cried from the entrance to the cave. "And all the buildings!"

"They were made with magic," Raval said, taking the Compact from Cindy in awe. "And the rules have changed."

"Now there *are* rules," Katy corrected.

"Are they good rules?" Danny wanted to know.

"I don't know if rules are really good or bad," Raval said honestly. "But they are the best rules we could come up with. It will matter how they are applied, I suppose. And that's up to you guys."

Randal was still reciting the first names of the kings and queens, his eyes closed. Katy touched his shoulder. "Randal?"

Randal's eyes flew open. "There are two of us now and we're *friends*." His face split into a brief grin and then went thoughtful and distant again.

"Let's shift!" Jamie hollered, and there was a moment of chaos as they forgot how big they would be as dragons and were too excited to heed the warnings from their partners and shifted too close together, cramming the mouth of the cave shut with interlocking dragon parts. Lancelot barked in a frenzy, confused and excited.

Katy thought that the dragons were smaller now than they'd been, if not as small as Raval's dragon. They had diminished, bonding with humans, and she wondered if they had any regrets. If they did, it was not apparent as they untangled themselves and frolicked outside, springing joyfully into the air with outspread wings.

She and Raval followed them, and Raval shifted himself to demonstrate flying technique and lead them in an obstacle course through the trees, dipping into the water and banking up the faces of the cliffs.

Katy watched from the ground, her face wet with happy tears.

At last, they all met again on the beach, each dragon

landing neatly, swirling sand with their wings. In a flicker, they were her children again, their faces glowing with bliss and they crowded forward to hug her.

"We're ready," Cindy said. "My dragon knows where we're going and how to get there. If we leave now, we'll be there before dark. Well, before dark *there*."

Katy hugged each of them and whispered good luck and last pieces of advice to each of them. "Remember that I love you. I'll tell Mackenzie you said hello and send your love. Go to bed on time. Be good to each other. Don't be too proud to ask for help. I *love* you."

And one by one, they took off, soaring up into the sky to vanish in a shimmer of not-quite-light.

Finally, only one dragon remained, Raval, and they were utterly alone on their side of the island.

CHAPTER 34

This, Raval thought, was what *empty-nester* meant.

Except that the nest itself was gone, too.

Not only had the children quite literally flown away, but the magic tents and everything that they had created from magic for their comfort was gone, as if it had never existed at all. The camp they'd laboriously eked out of the wilderness wouldn't be built for another century, or however long. The only thing that showed that anyone else had ever been there were the carved alcoves in the cave...and the car. Lancelot was racing around, whining and trying to figure out where everyone had gone. Occasionally, he would stop and dig into the sand, like he was worried that he'd buried them by mistake.

"It's all completely unreal," Katy said, wrapping her arms around herself.

Raval thought about testing his comedic timing by saying *there, there* again, but decided that it wasn't going to be funny that many times in a row, so he only wrapped his arms around Katy. "I'm going to miss playing king of the dragon," he admitted.

"There's still Dalaya," Katy reminded him.

Oh, his niece. Dalaya. It was strange to remember her, to remember the time that they'd come from at all. Raval thought he might have to try playing with her when they returned. Children hadn't been nearly the terror as he'd built them up in his mind. He was actually looking forward to one of his own. "Oh!" he realized with a start.

"What is it?" Katy asked.

"I might still have to really be king. Unless they've got that all figured out back in the right time."

"And I'd have to be queen," Katy said in surprise. "I'd almost forgotten." She tilted her head to one side. "But I suppose if we can ask those kids to be kings and queens, we have to be willing to step up and do it ourselves, as well."

"They won't be crowned for a while," Raval said. "We could probably stay here longer if you wanted. I'm not really sure how we'd contact them, but I could fly them down, probably."

"I'm ready to go home," Katy said plaintively. She had a hand over her belly. Not like it pained her, exactly, but like she was keenly aware of it.

Raval thought that he ought to say that home was wherever she was, but feared that it would fall flat. She knew that he loved her. He knew that she loved him. No one was expecting poetry.

They walked down to the beach one last time, looking at all the places that had been home, touching the trees that had endured both the times they had lived there. "Remember the first fire you lit?" Katy said, pointing to the fire pit.

"I felt a little bad," Raval admitted. "The kids had been trying so hard."

"And I told you about the baby on the driftwood bench just there."

"A baby!" It still felt like a bit of a shock every time he thought about it. "Your baby. My baby. A baby we made!"

"I remember making that baby," Katy said, smiling sideways at him. Was it a sly smile?

"Do you?" Raval asked in astonishment. "Which time was it?"

She laughed. "I can't know exactly," she teased him. "It might have been in our tent. Or in the car. Or that time we snuck off while the kids were fishing…"

"That night we went swimming?" Raval suggested. "Or that afternoon we sent them all searching for imaginary purple shells?"

They didn't recreate all of them, exactly, but they did realize that there were no children to avoid, and no reason to be quiet or sneaky. They could be as loud and exuberant and slow as they wanted…and Raval was surprised by how loud and exuberant and slow they could actually be. It was a whole new kind of sex, and Raval vowed to make sure that they could do it again. Maybe he could rent an entire island for privacy, when they were in their own time again. Or he could build them a cabin in the mountains.

"When do you want to go back?" he asked, when they were spent and sitting naked in the sun while their hair and clothing dried after swimming to clean off. Lancelot was snoozing beside them, worn out from playing in the water and being chased away during sex.

"Now?" Katy asked plaintively. "There's nothing left here, and I'd really love a hot shower and new clothing. The clock struck midnight and my ballgown has turned back into rags."

"I got that reference," Raval told her with a little smile. "Do you want a pumpkin ride home?"

"I'd like a mint green pumpkin coach ride now, please," Katy agreed, nudging Lancelot awake with one foot.

They dressed in their barely damp clothing, pausing to

appreciate each other and soak up one last sun-warmed hug before they walked up the trail to the cave for the last time.

Lancelot romped ahead of them and jumped willingly into the back seat of the car. Raval didn't even wince when his claws hit the leather seats.

Katy slid into the passenger seat and put her purse in her lap. "Ready?"

Raval turned the key in his hands but paused before putting it into the ignition.

He'd spent so much of his life thinking that he had to fix things. His mother's death. His own off-kilter head. He had harbored so much guilt and regret that he hadn't spent more time being selfless, that he couldn't do big public works like Fask, or write inspiring speeches like Rian, or even make people laugh like Tray.

But now he thought that the biggest fix that he'd actually needed was to accept himself, with all his quirks and qualities. It took driving them all back in time and setting destiny in motion to make him realize that he was absolutely fine, just the way he was, doing the best that he could. It was unreasonable of him to ask more of himself than anyone else did and it was only his failure to see what he *could* do that had kept him from doing it.

And there was Katy, the mirror that showed him all the ways to love himself, ready to go anywhere that he took her.

"I already fixed it," he said out loud, and he didn't have to put the key in the car at all for it to suddenly jolt to life, all of the lights on the dash coming on at once as the engine roared and the cave around them shattered.

CHAPTER 35

Katy found herself putting her hands over her belly protectively as the car jolted and shuddered and shook. She had to clench her eyes shut against the cacophony of light and when she dared to open them again, she had only a moment to feel relief at the sight of the garage that they'd left so many months prior before there were piercing lights flashing and a siren wailing. The front of the car was smoking more alarmingly than ever and the paint on the hood was bubbling as they watched.

Intruder! Intruder! Intruder! A mechanical voice overlaid the blaring siren.

Lancelot howled in chorus and Katy would have pressed her hands over her ears if she wasn't so busy with them trying to exit the car that was possibly on *fire*.

"Did your garage have this security system when we left?" Katy shouted.

Raval looked like he was in physical pain. "No! Argh! What the hell?! How does it turn off?"

They had barely gotten out of the car before the doors to the garage were flung open and a dozen of gun- and spear-wielding uniformed officers were spilling in to surround them, shouting directives. Katy put her hands up and accidentally let go of Lancelot's leash, so that he shot out into the crowd, eager to make friends. "Don't shoot him!" she cried in horror as several of them aimed in alarm.

"Hold your fire!" Raval roared, his voice full of power and authority.

"That's my line!"

Last into the garage was Captain Luke. She didn't appear to be armed, but Katy knew better than to think she was harmless. "Lower your weapons!" She inserted herself between her guards and bowed her head to Raval. "Your Highness."

The guards looked confused and Katy dashed forward to collect Lancelot, who had selected the nearest officer to lick his hand and wriggle for pets at his knee. She realized belatedly how they must look, in their very obviously ship-wrecked and worn-for-months clothing. She'd lost a lot of weight and gained a lot of muscle, even if she was still pretty curvy, and Raval was at least three shades darker than he'd been when they left. His hair had bleached to a Californian blond, besides being shoulder length, and he'd grown a full beard. It was really no wonder that they hadn't been recognized. Even Lancelot looked like a different dog, without any of his puppy fat or winter coat left. His tongue lolled out of the side of his mouth as Katy got ahold of what was left of the leash.

"What's with the security?" Raval shouted. "Can it be turned off?"

Either Captain Luke had a remote, or someone was watching through cameras that Katy hadn't remembered seeing before, because the siren finally went quiet and the obnoxious flashing of the lights stopped. It still felt weirdly, artificially light, and there were all sorts of mechanical sounds and fans and humming lights that Katy had never noticed before she spent several months without them.

Someone had a fire extinguisher, and stepped forward to deploy it when Raval popped the hood, hissing at the pain of the hot metal; it was apparently hot enough to hurt even him. The engine made several alarming groaning sounds in the relative silence as it cooled and the licking flames were smothered. Katy guessed that coming all the way to modern times in one jump had been harder on the car than it had been making two jumps into the past.

The smoke managed to trigger a smoke detector just then and the quiet from the security alarm was short lived.

It was a few moments of chaos and a cold draft from the open garage door before the alarm was silenced and anyone could speak again.

"Where are the kids?" Captain Luke wanted to know. "You failed?"

"It's a long story," Raval said, fanning the remains of the smoke away from the engine with a hand so that he could peer down at the smoldering remains of his life's work.

"How long have we been gone?" Katy wanted to know.

"You've been gone for three months!"

Katy wished she had a better handle on how long they'd been in Mo'orea. Had it only been three months? Had it been more?

A second wave of people was coming in the open garage door as the guards were dismissed and no one seemed to hear her question. Mackenzie was one of the first in this group, and she came and looked hopefully into the car windows, her despair almost palpable when she found it empty. "You didn't find them?"

"Where have you been?" Toren wanted to know, near her heels. "Look how tanned you are, Raval!"

"And shaggy," Rian added. Each of the brothers greeted Katy politely and gave Raval a very swift hug.

"And smelly," Tray added. "Lancelot!"

Lancelot leaped for Tray's face and licked and wiggled and jumped as if he had learned absolutely nothing in the months that Katy had been trying to train him.

Leinani asked gravely, "Are you...hurt?"

Katy saw the princess's gaze flicker to her waist, but it didn't linger there. Katy wasn't sure how much she was showing yet; perhaps it was just a coincidence.

Carina didn't give either of them a chance to answer, bounding in for a warm hug. "We'd given up on seeing you again! Where have you been *hiding*? Did they not have phones on your tropical vacation?"

"No one knew where you'd gone," Fask said crossly. "Or whether you'd come back."

"We're not hurt," Raval said, sharing a stiff hug with Fask, who was the last to arrive and looked very put out. "And the kids are fine."

Mackenzie looked into the back of the car again, like she thought they might be hiding there. "Where are they?"

Katy exchanged a look with Raval and the rest of the peppering conversation died down as they waited for an answer to the most pressing of the questions.

"They're...in the past," Katy tried to explain. She cast a look at Raval. She'd known these people barely three days before she'd gone on her time traveling adventure.

"Past what?" Mackenzie demanded. "Past where?"

"Past when," Raval clarified. "They are the eleven founding rulers of the Small Kingdoms."

The room went silent except for the sounds of machinery, still loud and unfamiliar to Katy's ears. She sighed, because Raval was either going to elaborate in great, unnecessary detail, or say nothing else at all. She explained briefly, "We went back in time, twice. We spent two months, give or take, roughing it with the kids on an abandoned beach on Mo'orea, and then we went back even further, to the writing of the Compact, met the first dragons, saved the world from a magical war, and might have invented the scientific method."

"This sounds like a very long story," Fask said at last, clearing his throat. "Perhaps we should do this inside. Or at least close the damned garage door. We don't need to pay to heat all of Alaska."

"C-can I get a shower first?" Katy asked plaintively. "Maybe a taco? I feel sick." She was suddenly very tired and near tears as the adrenaline ebbed away and she was starting to shiver violently.

Raval left the car and came to wrap his arms around her comfortingly. If his brothers were surprised by the easy and affectionate gesture, they were polite enough not to tease him.

"Of course," Leinani said immediately. "We'll have Mrs. James call in an order. Let's get you some fresh clothing and a drink. Water, or something stronger?"

"Just some water." Grateful for Raval's warmth, Katy let them fuss all of them together back to the castle.

"We have a lot of questions," Fask said, as they hurried through the snow to the main building. Carina wrapped her coat around Katy and someone put a hat on her head. The cold didn't bother Raval. They both had bare feet, but probably wouldn't get frostbite on the short trip. It wasn't as cold outside as it had been when they left—there was a promise of spring in the air and the snow had slumped and developed a sheen on top.

"And we have a lot of news," Kenth added, sounding satisfied as he hauled open the door of the castle. "We found the traitor and captured Amara. You missed a lot of excitement."

"Who?!" Raval demanded.

The uneasy quiet that answered him suggested to Katy that they knew Raval wasn't going to like the answer.

"Tell me later," Raval said shortly. "We have a lot of catching up to do on both sides." His hand in hers was the only thing that felt right to Katy. The cool dry air gave everything this tight, weird feeling of surreality after so long on the warm, humid island.

Lancelot had a spasm of uncertainty, torn between going with them and following Tray. "You remember your brother and sisters?" Tray said coaxingly, finally dragging him away. "I've got kibbles!"

Raval's rooms were a warm, magical escape after their long absence and Katy went willing with him into his enchanted bathroom.

"I am never putting these on again," Katy declared, peeling off her thoroughly worn-out clothing. Her underwear had more holes than whole fabric now and one of the legs had lost all of its elastic property such that it was constantly creeping into her butt.

She let Raval herd her into the big shower and turn on the not-magical-but-close-enough rain heads. There was real soap, after so long using gritty ash and fat, and Katy cleaned herself frantically the first time, then more slowly the second time, reveling in the feeling of being *really* clean again after so long.

She might have stayed in much longer, soaping herself and Raval's beautiful, perfect body, if hunger had not driven her out. They didn't use the magic spell to suspend the water droplets, too invested in using the flow to wash away the last of their sand and dirt and sweat.

Katy hadn't thought ahead to her clean clothes, but someone else had and when they emerged from the bathroom wrapped in a towel that she was already imagining a hundred vital uses for (a blanket, a filter, a hundred patches, a sun shade…), there was a steaming covered platter waiting in the sitting room with Katy's luggage.

She dressed swiftly, marveling in the amazing feeling of clean cloth against her skin. She didn't realize that she was crying until Raval drew her down in a chair and put the platter before her. "Eat," he insisted, removing the lid. It looked like tacos, but it didn't smell like tacos. Then he added, "Oh, sorry."

"For what?" Katy said, trying to remember what her silverware did.

"It's fish."

CHAPTER 36

Raval was so glad to hear Katy laugh about the tacos that he didn't even care that they were eating fish again after months of little else. It was spiced and breaded in ways that they'd never managed, and served with thick fries that they all but fought over, dipped in mayonnaise and ketchup and tartar sauce, scooping the last of it out of the serving containers with their fingers and licking them with an utter disregard for manners. They washed it all down with a tall glass of soda with ice cubes.

"Ice cubes!" Katy exclaimed, poking them down and watching them bob up again. "I had completely forgotten about ice cubes."

"It's late," Raval said, when they had both eaten themselves nearly to discomfort. He couldn't remember the last time he'd felt so full. "We don't have to meet the others right now. It can all wait until morning." It was bizarre to realize that just that day, they had witnessed the forming of the Compact and said farewell to the children that he'd come to be so fond of. It felt like they were in a whole different world, let alone a different time and he was having trouble wrapping his mind around it. It was all so illogical.

And maybe that was okay. Not everything had to be so rigid and defined, he'd learned. Not when there was someone like Katy to make everything okay.

She was gazing longingly into the bedroom. "I would like nothing more than to slide into your thousand-count sheets against your body and sleep for about a week," she admitted.

Raval knew there was a 'but' before she said it.

"But they deserve answers," Katy said with a tired sigh. "Mackenzie especially. And I'll admit, I am wild with curiosity. Who is the traitor? How did they capture Amara? What did they think when they realized the children were gone? I'm too wound up to sleep."

Raval remembered the etched glass that First had given him and went to make sure that he still had it, putting it into his pocket. *It will tell you the truth.*

They took their dishes with them when they left, and handed them to a guard who told them that the rest of the family was waiting in the library.

It was a lot of people for the space, all six brothers and five mates, plus Drayger, sprawled in a chair like he owned it, but Raval didn't find that he felt confined. He felt...like he was home.

Carina greeted Katy with a quick, kind hug and gave her a seat next to Mackenzie. Raval squeezed onto the couch next to her but didn't mind the feel of her thigh against his.

Mackenzie had a history textbook open on her lap. "I can't believe I didn't see it," she said.

There was a painting that spanned both pages and there they were, all eleven of them, dressed in robes and crowns, smiling for the portrait artist. The Compact lay on the table before them and they each held ink pens. Cindy's hair was in its kinky black curls and Danny had more than grown into his promise of height. The painter had deftly captured Randal's cool, distant look, and Lon's crooked grin. Jamie looked even more like Mackenzie than she had as a child. Most of the men had beards, the women had curves, some of them even had gray hair, but they were unmistakably the boys and girls that Katy had left behind in the past that very day, half a lifetime later.

They were the first kings and queens of the Small Kingdoms, chins high. They'd each taken the chance that was offered to them, united their countries, earned their crowns, and saved the world from a magical war that would have burned it down.

"They missed you," Katy told Mackenzie, slinging an arm around her shoulder. "They loved you so much, and I know that they hoped they would see you again."

"I guess I got to see *them*," Mackenzie said with a tearful little chuckle. "I'm so happy to know that they succeeded, that they always had each other, that they did so much with their lives. They would never have fit in here completely, it would have been so hard for them."

Katy grasped her up in a big, rocking hug that Mackenzie gradually relaxed into. Raval felt a little out of place and uncomfortable. "I have so many stories to tell you. And photos! I wasn't sure if it would, I don't know, break the timeline or violate history, but we had a little solar charger and I took so many photos on my phone."

"I can't wait to see them," Mackenzie said. "I want to know everything..." she burst into tears and clung to Katy.

"There, there," Kenth, sitting on her other side, said awkwardly as he patted her shoulder.

Raval shared a look with him over Katy and Mackenzie.

"How did you capture Amara?" Raval asked.

"Drayger was the hero of the hour," Fask said grudgingly, which sort of explained why the Majorcan bastard prince was in the library with the rest of them...and sort of didn't.

"All in the line of duty," Drayger said breezily. "I had a few contacts that were able to get us ahead of her for once."

"Who was it in the palace that was helping her?"

The faces that met his were all confusing but Raval was pretty sure that there was grief or anger or betrayal involved. He wasn't sure which of those emotions were key...or if it was all of them.

"Nathaniel," Fask finally said, sounding deeply conflicted.

Raval glanced at Tray. Nathaniel was in charge of the dog yard, and one of Tray's closest friends. He'd always been trusted by their father and had been a source of comfort and advice when his long slumber first began. It felt...unlikely... that he would have any part of kidnapping children and betraying the royal family. Was this another sign that Raval's judgment was suspect? He remembered the glass coin in his pocket. It would tell him the truth, but it was meant to tell him the truth about his father. Should he use it for a more immediate good, or should he just trust that the correct culprit had been caught?

Fask told the story of Amara's capture, punctuated by Toren's enthusiastic embellishment and Kenth's disapproving corrections. Raval barely followed it, not as interested in the how as he was in the end result. Amara was imprisoned, the residue of her cult was dissolving without the magic she'd used to hold it together, Fask was using all the means he had to get magic back in the bag, Kenth was certain he couldn't, and the Renewal was galloping down on them in just weeks—and they still didn't know who to send.

"Your return means there are still five choices," Fask said to Raval. Sourly?

"We've already done one Renewal," Katy said merrily. "Does that mean he gets a free pass?" Mackenzie had pulled herself together and the history book was shut in her lap, though she continued to pet it as if it were a cat companion.

"It doesn't count as a Renewal if it's the first one," Raval said, knowing he sounded pedantic but not quite able to stop himself.

Katy didn't seem to mind. "But it sounds like a happy ending, then? You've toppled the Cause and we can leave the castle safely again?"

But Fask was frowning. "Not exactly. There have been more attempts on the Compact and on members of the monarchies since Amara was captured. We thought it was just members of the Cause trying one last hurrah, but there may be other players involved. It's possible that someone else is angling to prevent the Renewal, for the same reasons."

Raval chewed on the idea of unlimited magical power available again. He could see the appeal of it, even if he knew too intimately now the reasons that it had been structured in the first place. Greedy and power-hungry people would not hesitate to use it for their own purposes.

And they still didn't know why the Compact had called more than one mate for Alaska. Had the dragons added that only because they already knew it would happen? Or was it something that the Compact, once self-aware, had decided for itself?

Raval only knew that he was desperately glad it had chosen Katy for him, because he could not imagine happiness without her now.

She stirred uncomfortably at his side and stood up. "I hope you'll excuse me," she said. "I really, really have to use the little princess room."

Everyone stared at Raval when she'd left the room, giving him a quick kiss before she went, and there was a pause while he tried to figure out why.

"Is she...?"

Tania didn't finish, but Leinani did, asking bluntly, "Is she pregnant?"

A baby! Katy's baby! His baby! A baby they *made!* It wasn't that Raval had forgotten, he had just forgotten that they might not know. He wondered if it showed in the lines of Katy's body, but she'd always been curvy, and he couldn't really tell.

"Yes," he said, far more calmly than he felt.

That stirred up a hum of conversation and congratulations and practical suggestions. "I have about a hundred tests that they keep leaving in my bathroom as subtle hints," Carina said. "I can give her a dozen and not miss them."

"Mrs. James will be so happy!"

"We should have a baby shower!"

"Give them a little space, they've been wrecked on an island for several months."

"Well, that is one way to make babies..."

"Maybe this will mean people will finally lay off," Carina muttered.

"Don't bet on it, Your Highness." Toren didn't sound terribly sympathetic.

Kenth clapped him on the shoulder so hard Raval was sure he'd have a bruise. Fask's congratulations felt practiced, though probably he'd practiced it for one of their other brothers.

Raval didn't need a mate bond in order to know that Katy was taken aback when she returned to a library full of people that tried very hard not to stare at her. Everyone took very suspiciously timed sips of their drinks and there was an awkward moment when no one was exactly sure what to say, and then she laughed and said in exasperation, "Well, I'm guessing you all know, then? It's a good thing this palace has a hundred bathrooms because I'm not even showing yet and I already have to pee every twenty minutes."

That led to laughter and another, warmer, round of congratulations, this one filled with hugs and more enthusiastic questions.

"I'm fine, I'm fine," Katy assured them. "I'd love to get a good night's sleep on a bed with an actual pillow and actual sheets, and toilet paper is an unspeakable luxury, but it isn't like we starved!"

She promised to have a doctor look her over anyway and Raval didn't think that her yawns were fabricated as he dragged her back to his rooms.

"It's been a long day," she said, letting him tuck her into his bed. He kissed her, but didn't press for more; there would be plenty of time for that later and she was clearly exhausted. "Don't tuck me in too tight," she cautioned drowsily. "I'll just have to get up and pee."

She was asleep in moments, while Raval was still pulling the drapes shut so that she could sleep as long as she wanted. He wasn't sure when the sun would rise. When they'd left, the sun was down long into the day, but later in the season, dawn would be earlier and even the night could be bright with moonlight on snow.

He paused to look down at her, her face slack in slumber and her hair splayed over her pillow.

It was so remarkable to see her and know that she was his, that she was carrying their child, that their adventure was finally over and they were safe home in the castle at the right time at last.

They'd been through so much, so fast, that it felt like Raval was taking a deep breath for the first time in a long while, like he'd been diving deep and had finally surfaced for air.

There was just one thing that he had left to do…

CHAPTER 37

Raval didn't remember the castle so crawling with guards. For so much of his life, it had been just him and his brothers, plus a skeleton staff run iron-handed by Mrs. James. The royal guards had been spread across the state, as much for image as for protection.

But Fask had started recalling them to close duty when Toren first brought Carina home and there was an attempt on their lives. And since then, it had only gotten more frenetic, with attempts on the Compact, incursions right into their very vault and their bedrooms.

Now, there were guards at every door and corridor crossing. Raval longed for the days of quiet hallways and no *people*.

The guards at the stairs down to the vault started to challenge him, then recognized him and let him pass. Raval bit back his impulse to explain what he was doing and walked down the broad stairs to the tunnel below. It was oddly comforting to have stone walls around him. The cave had been part of their home for so long. This was well-lit, though, and perfectly smooth and polished.

Randal must have helped make this corridor, Raval realized. Not immediately, perhaps, but early in his reign, he would have created the vault and set the spells that protected it, tied to the Compact and renewed when it was. He trailed his hand along the big doors to the vault...and went past it.

There was one door before the end and Raval paused there a moment. This would be where Amara and Nathaniel were held, warded impenetrably against escape or communication. He wondered if they were enspelled on top of the constraints of the prison, if they had regrets, whether they would live their lives out in their dungeon.

He went on to the door at the end.

It was as large and heavy as the door to the vault but when he placed his hand on it and said his full name, *Paravalitenek*, it swung open soundlessly, with no more pressure than it took to brush aside a leaf.

Raval almost went into the darkness, then remembered that he wasn't still stuck in prehistory; they had light switches here.

The overhead lights were jarring, uncomfortably bright but Raval shut the door behind him and went in anyway.

"Father," he said solemnly to the mountain of a sleeping dragon.

He'd never been as close with his father as he'd been with his mother, but he had fond memories of the man's strength and humor. He'd been a good ruler, and a good father, fair and even-handed. The story for the public, once it was clear that he wasn't making appearances, was that he was desperately ill. Medical coma was a term that Raval had seen used, and he wasn't sure if it was Fask's idea or if the media had come to that themselves, but they knew that he was in a fugue state where they couldn't declare a death and hold a funeral, but where they also had to accept that it was time for a new ruler.

Of course, the media didn't realize that the Dragon King's coma was in his literal dragon form.

Raval fingered the disc of glass in his pocket. Perhaps his father's sleep really *was* only grief, or exhaustion. Perhaps there was no ulterior motive or hidden agenda to it. Perhaps it was only natural. He was old, by now, and though dragons lived longer than most humans, was pushing the end of his expected lifespan. He'd found his mate and fathered his children late in his life.

Should he use the truth stone for some better purpose than to satisfy his own curiosity? Did it have more than one use in it? Would it matter *why* his father slept if Raval couldn't actually wake him? Certainly he'd tried before, spending weeks on spells that only sputtered and failed, wasting time on flawed magic without enough understanding. Maybe knowing what trapped him in this state could help Raval solve the issue.

Raval drew out the glass and held it up at arm's length. "Truth," he said, only at that moment remembering that it was one of the six virtues of the Small Kingdoms. He wondered, fleetingly, if there were spells for the other five.

For a moment nothing happened. There was no sound, this deep in the earth, except for the annoying buzz of the recessed lighting and the agonizingly slow rhythm of his father's breath and quiet heartbeat.

Had First miscalculated the requirements of magic after the Compact had restrained it? The car had worked, but perhaps this would not.

There was a tiny swirl of light, deep in the glass and Raval brought it closer to his eye curiously. There wasn't a picture inside of it, exactly, but when he held it close, he could look through it at an overlay of this room, and as he swung it back and forth, he could see strands of power that wrapped his father's jaw and strapped his wings to his side.

This wasn't a natural sleep. The magical bonds dived into the king's body itself, binding his heart and squeezing his lungs. "Who did this?" Raval asked in horror. Was this Amara's work? It would have been one of her first acts of magic, if he remembered the timeline correctly. But she would have needed someone in the palace to work such a spell. Was Nathaniel even capable of such magic? His skill with dogs bordered on sorcery, but Raval and his dragon had never felt even a sniff of magic from him.

As if driven by his thoughts, the view through the glass changed, tilting dizzily and Raval stared in horror at what it showed him...

The story concludes in *The Dragon Prince's Betrayal!*

A NOTE FROM ELVA BIRCH

Thank you for reading *The Dragon Prince's Magic*! I had so much fun writing about Katy and Raval and I can't wait to return to this world for the big series finale!! (I am very much hoping to have it out sooner than the current preorder date —that's my everything-goes-wrong date and I've already started writing it.) A huge thank you to my editors, and to my sensitivity readers. It was important to me to make sure I represented neurodivergence in a healthy, respectful way and I am grateful to the people who were willing to read an early version to make sure I was on the right track.

Your reviews are very much appreciated; I read them all and they help other readers decide whether or not to buy my books! Thank you to all of my fabulous beta readers and copy editors; any errors that remain are entirely my own. If you do find any typos — or you'd just like to share your thoughts with me! — feel free to email me at elvaherself@elvabirch.com. My cover was designed by Ellen Million.

To find out about my new releases, you can follow me on Amazon, subscribe to my newsletter, or like me on

A NOTE FROM ELVA BIRCH

Facebook. Join my Reader's Retreat on Facebook for sneak previews and cut scenes. Find all the links at my webpage: elvabirch.com

I also write under other pen names—keep reading for information about my other available titles...

MORE BY ELVA BIRCH

A Day Care for Shifters: A hot new full-length series about adorable shifter kids and their struggling single parents in a town full of mystery and surprise. Start the series with Wolf's Instinct, when Addison comes to Nickel City to take a job at a very special day care and finds a family to belong to. A gentle ice-cream-straight-from-the-container escape. Sweet and sizzling!

* * *

The Royal Dragons of Alaska: A fascinating alternate world where Alaska is ruled by secret dragon shifters. Adventure, romance, and humor! Reluctant royalty, relentless enemies… dogs, camping, and magic! Start with The Dragon Prince of Alaska.

* * *

Suddenly Shifters: A hilarious series of novellas, serials, and shorts set in the small town of Anders Canyon, where something (in the water?) is making ordinary citizens turn into shifters. Start with Something in the Water! Also available in audio!

* * *

Birch Hearts: An enchanting collection of short stories and novellas. Unconstrained by theme or setting, each short read has romance, magic, and heart, with a satisfying conclusion. And always, the impossible and irresistible. Start with a sampler plate in Prompted 2 for fourteen pieces of sweet-to-sizzling flash fiction, or dive in with the novella, Better Half. Breakup is a free story!

WRITING AS ZOE CHANT

Shifting Sands Resort: A complete ten-book series - plus two collections of shorts. This is a sizzling shifter romance set at a tropical island resort. Each book stands alone but connects into a great mystery with a thrilling conclusion. Start with Tropical Tiger Spy or dive in to the Omnibus edition, with all of the novels, short stories, and novellas in my preferred reading order! This series crosses over with *Fire and Rescue Shifters* and *Shifter Kingdom!*

* * *

Fae Shifter Knights: A complete four-book fantasy portal romp, with cute pets and swoon-worthy knights stuck in a world of wonders like refrigerators and ham sandwiches. Start with Dragon of Glass!

* * *

Green Valley Shifters: A sweet, small town series with single dads, secret shifters, sweet kids, and spinsters. Lowperil and steamy! Standalone books where you can revisit your favorite characters—this series is also complete! Start with Dancing Barefoot! Green Valley Shifters crosses over with **Virtue Shifters**. Start with Timber Wolf!

THE BOOK I'M NOT WRITING

Writing as Elva Birch
She's got one life to live

Anita takes a chance at a job she's not sure she can handle and she's tickled pink when the gorgeous billionaire picks her little bakery to cater his big charity event. But what was supposed to be the opportunity of a lifetime turns into the storm of a century.

He's got one leg to stand on

Frank Wilson has built his reputation and his world-spanning lawn ornament business on one tenet: honesty. There's nothing fake about Frank Wilson -- not his fabulous fortune or his amazing physique.

...or his inner flamingo.

Trapped together with his fated mate in his big empty office building with two thousand gourmet cupcakes and no power, Frank is sure that -- finally -- nothing will stand between him and everything that he'd ever wanted, in the arms of a curvy woman wearing an apron. The only problem is, she's not interested in settling down to join his flock.

And to win her heart, he's going to have to put his foot down.

* * *

I love to do harmless April Fool's Day pranks, and I made this cover for my readers, even going so far as to make a book blurb and fake Amazon book preview image for Facebook.

But the joke's on me and this, of all of the books I have planned, is the one I have the most readers clamoring for!

I am not writing it. I am not writing the scene where Anita plays Simon Says and makes Frank stand on one foot forever. I am not plotting the chapter where they are dancing around the empty ballroom. I am not researching all the flamingo jokes on the internet.

If you would like to read more of the book I'm very definitely not writing, or its sequels, you'll have to sign up for my mailing list at elvabirch.com or join Elva Birch's Readers Retreat at Facebook!

A PREVIEW OF TROPICAL TIGER SPY

When Amber booked her vacation at Shifting Sands Resort, she was expecting a lazy tropical vacation at a luxury escape for shifters...she wasn't expecting to meet a sexy under-cover tiger shifter spy who set her blood on fire, or to become a part of his investigation into why shifters are disappearing from the resort! An excerpt of Tropical Tiger Spy.

Amber walked meekly with the guards, trying not to be too obvious about looking around. The dog-catcher was lying unexpectedly loose at her shoulders, and when she glanced at the man holding the pole, he glared back and fingered a button on the handle. The other guard, walking behind her with the gun trained on her, cleared his throat, and Amber put her head down and continued to shamble with them. She was short, so it was easy to walk slowly and look like she was using a normal pace.

The looseness of the noose around her neck got her brain spinning.

They were expecting a mountain cat—an American mountain cat. A *big* mountain cat. If she shifted, the dog-catcher would be tight around the neck of a big cat. But around her small cat shape...

As quickly as the idea occurred to her, Amber put it in motion, shifting as she pretended to stumble.

Her clothing fell away from her cat form even as she jumped—straight through the noose—and scrambled for the wall of the mesh enclosure they were walking past. She heard the crackle of the dog-catcher rather than feeling it through her thick fur, and realized belatedly that it must be electrified. She wasn't sure if she would have made this attempt if she'd known that, but it was far too late now, and her coat, meant for cold mountain winters, had protected her from the worst of it.

She climbed in a panic, the agility of her cat form driving her, and as the guard behind her fired and missed, and missed again as she switched directions up the enclosure and reached the roof.

She heard the zoo erupt into roars and animal cries of encouragement. A human voice even cried out, "Go, kitty cat!"

"Shit!" the guards said in unison.

More wild shots followed her. Needles hissed by as Amber made it up to the roof of the enclosure. She ran and leaped to the next. She was already two cages away while the guards were still peering up onto the first. Then she switched directions entirely and leaped across the path to a new row of cages.

Her night sight let her see better than she had as a human, and her height gave her a clear view. Lights all along the wall had come on, showing her that she had no real chance of getting over them—though she could probably squeeze between the barbed wire with little damage thanks to her coat, she was too small to make it to the top of the wall to try; nothing was built up close to it. She noticed the cameras, too, now swiveling back into the enclosure to try to find her, and had a glimpse of a helicopter on one of the low roofs towards the back.

"Goddamn it, do you see it?" one guard called to the other.

"Beehag said it was a mountain cat, not a goddamn *little* cat!" the other complained.

Their voices were clear to Amber's excellent hearing.

Instead of immediate escape, Amber looked for hiding spaces, and found one in a pile of construction materials towards the end of the zoo. While the cameras were still repositioning to try to follow her, she dashed out of sight down the side of one of the enclosures and flattened herself to fit in a tiny space on top of a pile of rocks, under dimension lumber and roof tiles. From here, she could see a dozen more hiding places that she'd be able to make it to in short order, and she had a good vantage for seeing oncoming intruders.

She could actually see that the entire zoo was actually much more suited for containing big animals. She'd be able to get out, she felt, with her first taste of confidence as the adrenaline began to release its hold on her. She just had to lie low, and she'd be able to sneak out of the front gates when the timing was right.

"Call it in!" one of the guards was saying.

"Fuck no, you call it in," the other protested.

Eventually, they worked out who was making the call, and the little two-way radio crackled in return as they explained their mistake.

"Escaped?" Even over the poor quality radio from a distance, Amber recognized Alistair's voice, and it made the hackles on her neck rise.

The guards fell over each other to justify their actions, and Amber gave a little cat smile to hear them describe her as basically supernatural.

A PREVIEW OF TROPICAL TIGER SPY

There was a moment of silence in response, and then Alistair's crisp accent. "She won't get far. We've got her *mate* here."

Mate?

Amber knew without a doubt that they meant Tony, and it was everything she could do not to bolt from her hiding hole right then to find and defend him. But what did they mean by 'mate?' She could all but hear the emphasis that Alistair was putting on it.

The waiter at the resort had used the same word.

Whatever they meant by it, she knew that Alistair was right—knowing that they had Tony—that they might *hurt* Tony to get her, meant that Alistair had Amber as surely as if that noose *had* been tight around her neck.

Read the rest of *Tropical Tiger Spy* now!